Praise for *Beginning of Was*

"A beautiful book, honest, unflinching and sometimes almost unbearable in its intensity, yet in the end also hopeful and oddly buoyant."   —Nino Ricci, author of *Lives of the Saints* and *The Origin of Species*

"Rich with observations about the twists and turns in life … Szado's tale comes in a refreshing new voice."
—*Toronto Star*

"Szado's prose is restrained and powerful … It isn't just the story, compelling as it is. Szado evokes our own history of grief and loss and opens us to the fears that haunt our dreams. Ultimately, it is through her fiction that we come to understand how to proceed.   —*Ottawa Citizen*

"A lyrical evocation of grief, *Beginning of Was* explores the nature of the human heart with elegance and compassion."
—Helen Humphreys

"Szado's debut novel, *Beginning of Was,* tells an emotionally taut tale of trauma without clichés or sentimer' also knows how to ratchet up the tension … The of the year."   —*N(*

"This is an auspicious debut and a welcome ad range of contemporary Canadian novels that expl in the face of despair and loss."   —*N(*

"A sparingly written, subtle exploration of personal tragedy and how to survive it, how to cling on, as onto a rock face—slowly inching towards the possibility of a future."

—D.M. Thomas

"*Beginning of Was* is all touch. Ania Szado communicates the feeling of contact and makes a beautiful ache."

—Gord Downie, author of *Coke Machine Glow*

"Ania Szado shows once again how Canadian writers can portray with stunning virtuosity the telling details and little events that make a life."   —*The Hamilton Spectator*

"Szado shows an immense talent for resonant and surprising imagery."   —*Quill & Quire*

PENGUIN

BEGINNING OF WAS

ANIA SZADO's novel *Beginning of Was* was short-listed for the Commonwealth Writers' Prize (Best First Book, Canada/Caribbean), nominated for the international Kiriyama Prize, and named a *NOW* magazine Top Ten book. She lives in Toronto.

BEGINNING OF
Was

ANIA SZADO

PENGUIN
an imprint of Penguin Canada

Published by the Penguin Group
Penguin Group (Canada), 90 Eglinton Avenue East, Suite 700, Toronto, Ontario, Canada M4P 2Y3

Penguin Group (USA) Inc., 375 Hudson Street, New York, New York 10014, U.S.A.
Penguin Books Ltd, 80 Strand, London WC2R 0RL, England
Penguin Ireland, 25 St Stephen's Green, Dublin 2, Ireland (a division of Penguin Books Ltd)
Penguin Group (Australia), 707 Collins Street, Melbourne, Victoria 3008, Australia
(a division of Pearson Australia Group Pty Ltd)
Penguin Books India Pvt Ltd, 11 Community Centre, Panchsheel Park, New Delhi – 110 017, India
Penguin Group (NZ), 67 Apollo Drive, Rosedale, Auckland 0632, New Zealand
(a division of Pearson New Zealand Ltd)
Penguin Books (South Africa) (Pty) Ltd, 24 Sturdee Avenue, Rosebank,
Johannesburg 2196, South Africa

Penguin Books Ltd, Registered Offices: 80 Strand, London WC2R 0RL, England

Published in Penguin paperback by Penguin Canada, 2004
Published in this edition, 2013

1 2 3 4 5 6 7 8 9 10 (WEB)

LIBRARY AND ARCHIVES CANADA CATALOGUING IN PUBLICATION

Szado, Ania
Beginning of was / Ania Szado.

ISBN 978-0-14-301475-1

I. Title.

PS8637.Z23B43 2013   C813'.6   C2013-900336-3

Visit the Penguin Canada website at **www.penguin.ca**

Special and corporate bulk purchase rates available; please see
www.penguin.ca/corporatesales or call 1-800-810-3104, ext. 2477.

ALWAYS LEARNING   PEARSON

To Bruce, Ela, and Luke, with love

A POLICEMAN STOPPED THE TRAFFIC, and the traffic blocked the fire engine. The ambulance workers waited while the car burned a rectangle into the road.

There were flames: red and high, low and smouldering. Dark breath rolled out, churned to the road.

There were black tips of bones.

I stitched together the words of strangers, overheard on every street: *Tragic. Inconvenient. It made me so late. The gridlock, the stink. Air pollution. Spectacle.*

Burn, baby, burn. I heard it in every mouth.

I heard my voice. *Identify?* My child never looked like that, never smelled like that, never broke like that. She was strong, pink, alive. With eyes.

Asha could run, could open the car door, could would will come home.

But that other one, Officer, the one with the scorched teeth, that one was my husband, Kurt.

1

MRS. OLAND IS PACKING. My job last night was to steal newspapers from the animal shelter up the street. Now Mrs. Oland is on her stiff old knees in front of the dark china cabinet, wrapping crystal goblets in *The Urban Pet* and *Toronto Animal Rights Review*. The glasses squeak in protest as her bony hands push paper down their gullets. One has escaped; I've filled it with red wine. I'm taking a break.

"Be gentle," I say, cradling my glass.

Perhaps I should say, "Have respect," rub a wet finger slowly, insistently, around the rim, and watch Mrs. Oland's eyes widen as sound rises from the crystal to press against our ears—the sweet eerie song of the passage from living to dead. I do not. Mrs. Oland's time is too near, and my job is not to warn, but to watch and work.

I set down my goblet and reach for newsprint.

∽

My first morning with Mrs. Oland I struggled to adjust to her habit of inventory. She didn't need figures or fingertips to count her belongings. Their number, their volume, and their meaning were in her bones. But this was all new to me,

3

this reckoning. All I knew then was that Mrs. Oland needed to pack. She was not planning to move; she was planning to die—and to live on in her possessions.

She perched in an armchair and I tipped my head to hear.

"I've always been careful with my things. They're not chipped or stained like some people's."

On the mirrored shelf near her head, cut crystal animals sat in a thin film of dust.

"I chose them carefully, you know. People don't seem to realize that. They think I can give away my treasures and forget I ever had them. I won't forget them, Marta. I need my things."

"Then why pass them on now?"

"What would you have me do? I'm eighty-eight. Should I simply die and have my possessions snatched up by anyone who wants them?"

"You don't have a will?"

"A will! This is my will: that every one of my progeny thinks twice. When they get their bit of inheritance through the post, they'll find out what my will is. They might not understand right away, but eventually they'll see. No one who puts their hands on things like these isn't changed. And they shall be changed. That is my will."

And I am her witness.

Things assigned to people. Objects indivisible from their purposes, the missions they will accomplish. An artillery of objects and a field of unsuspecting victims.

Who was out there, unseen and unheard from? Who was hers? How many invisible offspring and unnamed relatives crowded the world like ghosts? Progeny, progenitors.

Beloveds. How many long-time or long-lost friends swam and glimmered in Mrs. Oland's memories? What was the meaning of the objects in this house?

In the kitchen, I bent to stare at the squashed faces of twelve Pekinese dog figurines cluttering a window ledge. I pulled the curtains open as far as they would go, giving the dogs a wider stage, and set the Pekes at equal distances to each other. Old kitchen residue dulled their backs. My fingers were tacky with it.

I took the dogs down, submerged them in soapy water, and thumbed the sticky grease off their flowing coats. Coats white, grey, blue-green, golden yellow, beige. The final ones to receive their scrubbings were pale yellow with painted gold accents, a family of three.

Thin chains of old brass linked the collars of the two flat-faced pups to their mother's. She sat high, thrusting out her chest, her lower jaw protruding, her ears perked as though snatched by the wind.

I held the group in my palm. I turned the mother over. There: the pups had been whelped from the hole in her base, complete with chains. Complete with navy-blue tattoos stamped on their rumps, "Made in Occupied Japan."

I laughed and sank my hands into the water. The trio tumbled together, clinking silently.

∾

Mrs. Oland and I wrap her possessions to be sent before her death to her relatives and friends. We work slowly and deliberately. She requests assistance or attention numerous times within each hour and rests for long stretches each day. This afternoon, weak sunshine trickles in through tired lace curtains. We finish packing a set of teacups and move on to breakfast dishes.

"So," Mrs. Oland says, "what do people eat for fancy breakfast these days?"

"I suppose some start with grapefruit."

"Small plates, then. Let's do the bright white ones with the beautiful cobalt edges. High up in the cabinet . . . above the vases."

Up I go. The dishes tremble against each other, against my chest, as I shift my weight.

"Shhh," I whisper, pulling them close, stepping carefully off the chair. I kneel on Mrs. Oland's Turkish rug and release the fragile plates onto the thin carpet. I divide the glossy stack between us, dealing plates.

"Nine, ten."

"I shall give the whole set to Ron's new baby," Mrs. Oland says. "Ron was an awful teenager. He hated having breakfast, and he ate with his hands." She lays out a sheet of newspaper. "But he won't be teaching his habits to the baby, not when the child has these lovely plates at home."

We each pick one up. They are cool to the touch. I press mine to my forehead then hold it away.

Blue-ringed, below an oval of my own human grease, the face in the plate stares back at me.

2

I GREW UP IN KINGSTON, three hours from Mrs. Oland's bungalow. Little left its mark on my very early years, except my mother's narrow back hunched over her sewing, her foot rising and falling to the thrum of the machine, her spine shifting against the hidden zipper of her dress.

Strangers stopped my stroller to offer my stern-faced mama words: "A girl? How old? How sweet."

Her German formations of tongue and teeth softened in this land of soft sounds. She told me so when I was six; I held a wrenched-out baby tooth. "'How old, how sweet,'" she repeated as blood pooled against my lip.

In my house we spoke English: mine natural, my father's mild and accented, my mother's exquisite and controlled. Sidling up against my father, reaching for my mother's indifferent fingers, I bounced with them—my immigrant parents—through all the early stages of real estate and respectability, and back again.

In a way it was perfect: a time of preparation for this, this aloneness, this adult life.

My father came and went, going to his patients, returning from his patients. He came home quiet. We lived in a house with an old bull-nosed wooden threshold which often tripped him up; still he entered tangled in thought, with his cache of words dragging below the surface.

Slowly he refocused. His voice as thick as sleep, he spilled a greeting—"Ah, Marta"—into the hallway along with his shoes. His eyes read our home in degrees. Grey-flecked carpet, loops leading to loops leading to rooms. Mint green walls: our living room, with armchair beckoning. Sweet, smoky smell, frying onions: dinner. Home. "Merisa, I'm home!" His voice rose up to my mother hesitantly. A voice like an offering.

My mother received it and gave to him a sigh, her hands pausing on half-sewn garments or pushing shreds of beef against sizzling strips of pepper, stabbing potatoes in their pot.

Back then Papa drove a family sedan with a bench seat wide enough for four children in the back. I was their only child: Marta Ostentuin, curly haired, curls loose and lazy and brown. My hair slumped down from a centre part then sprang up in wide, implausible arcs that bounced about my round face. I would hook my arms and soft chin over the car's front seat and peer down at my mother's hands. In the summertime she sat with her fine, strong fingers spread on the vinyl upholstery. Every few minutes she straightened the line of her side seams and adjusted the position of her puddling thighs.

My hands on the seat back fidgeted too, pulling up from the slick upholstery with the sound of a wet kiss, settling into a new damp grip near my mother's otter-brown hair. In the winter my fingers crept to her hat—a flattened globe of fur, laden in its depths with angel-soft down and bristling with gentle tickling spikes all around.

My father was a dentist. He worked with his bare hands against bloody gums, with saliva spouting and evaporating along the length of his fingers, which were steady then. He pushed needles into old, receding gums, while wincing and pressing his tongue to the same spot in his own mouth.

Whenever he filled my teeth, he lulled me to calmness with his soothing voice that muffled the drill's metallic whine.

"Imagine yourself on the beach, Marta, lying on the sand. Feel its warmth . . . Feel yourself warm and heavy on the sand, sinking into the sand, everything clear and pure and heavy as water, sinking . . ."

I would forget the violating drill bit, forget the embarrass-ment of my oversized horse-teeth and the pressure in my nervous bladder. I would lie awash in the antiseptic smell that misted in the beat of ocean waves. I would feel the surf in my torso, drawing me down. I would imagine my arms, too heavy to lift, lifting to my father who bent close to me, and my mouth, too drowsy to speak, murmuring, *Lie down, Papa, lie with me*.

I knew my father's ways with words, and with pain. I knew how they worked: I saw how an old man, one of my father's patients, heard Papa's soothing voice. How he let its seductive rhythms enter his exhausted heart. How he let that voice carry him across.

My mother told me the rest. My father told her, and she told me.

She was here then.

He talked then.

∞

The patient was Leonard, Old Leonard—but most of my father's patients were old. They were grandparents and great-grandparents, a contingent of Kingston's elders who had stubbornly kept their own teeth, protecting them as fiercely as they guarded their driver's licences, choosing their dentists as carefully and cautiously as they chose tins of dinner for their housecats. Perhaps they all knew each other, Kingston's seniors. It seemed they all talked, gossiped, shared news and advice. It seemed, for a time, they all chose my father.

In the summer Papa sometimes took me with him to his office. I would spend the morning in the waiting room, sprawled on the carpeted floor over a colouring book, near the stick-thin or swollen ankles of a seated patient. My own swinging feet were always in the way of the door. I was always forgetting myself and my place—gazing up the lengths of canes and stockinged or trousered legs as patients entered and waited for me to move.

Leonard was already in the hallway of the Medical Arts Building when we arrived that morning. He stood stooped and skinny outside the dental office door, breathing audibly, one long hand gripping the doorknob.

My father advanced with the key.

"Good morning, Leonard. You're bright and early. Marta, hold the door for Mr. Lenski." My father didn't look at people when he spoke to them.

That morning I sat in a chair. I leafed through magazines, closed my eyes, and listened to the murmurs from the procedure room. Once in a while I slipped out to steal a snapshot look at my father in his white dentist's coat, then swung back to my chair, ducking under the receptionist's sharp gaze.

My father's hand was at the old man's mouth, poking gently around a molar. The anaesthetic had taken effect, right down to a small drip that numbed part of the tongue.

"Tongue numb," Leonard said; these would be his last words.

My father nodded. He glanced at me, then prodded the tooth and picked up the drill.

"Leonard," my father began, with a discreet press of the trigger, "just imagine for a moment." He straightened briefly, gazing into the distance. His voice was soft and gentle. "Your body is relaxed, your mind is free. You can go anywhere from here. Your mind is an airplane. A ship. Let it glide you away, far from this room. These small adjustments to teeth . . . Teeth are only tools, things of the body. Don't let the body hold you back. You can go anywhere. Anywhere."

The patient sighed. The body shuddered. My father leaned in.

"Imagine this now: sunshine. Warm, healing sunshine comforting everything it touches. Sunshine warming a wide, empty beach. You're there, Leonard. Your feet are up. Your hands are folded on your chest, on a book."

He paused, working, concentrating.

Then, gently: "Your favourite book. You're drifting into an easy sleep. Safe, relaxed. Hear the waves. They go on and on. Your body is heavy on the warm sand . . ."

My father spoke and drilled. The drill's penetrating pitch raised the fine hairs on the back of my neck. But it did not bother Leonard.

Leonard's spirit had wrapped itself around my father's words. It had passed with them through the walls, seeped through the blinds and the window, lifted its face to the sun.

When my father stopped drilling, Leonard's mouth remained open. The old man's eyelids, heart, and breath were still. My father stood silently for a long time. Then he put out a hand, palm up, and cupped the jaw.

The story didn't make the papers; there was no need for that. It spread in tremulous whispers over psalm books, in bursts of indignation at chicken lunches, in frightened prayers cast into the air. It slipped from between knobby knuckles and entered straining ears. It passed from person to person, hand to mouth, mouth to hand. It even made it to my playground, contorted and grotesque.

My father lost his practice. He watched his patients shift and fade away, stealthily and steadily, like the saliva he'd tracked through their wrinkles.

His patients were too old to take chances. They wanted to live.

There was nothing official. My father was not stripped of his licence. He was stripped of his living.

My mother sewed. She was a wonder. A sewing wonder. A seamstress. The best there was. Women said so as they stood in our dining room with fingers feeling for the side button of a skirt or reaching for the bow at the throat of a silk blouse, then they stared at me until I left the room.

Sometimes I waited on the front porch, my thick, five-year-old's fingers bending the tabs of paper clothing over the shoulders of cardboard dolls. From there I could see my father. My father sat in the car.

I would wait until the day's smugly smiling customer clipped past me in her flat boots or square, late-sixties heels, then slip back to my mother's side.

"Can I help? Please?"

"Not now."

"Please, Mama? Is this the side seam or the—"

"Don't touch! Here, this is going to be the cuff. See this stitching? Take it apart, just to where this pin is. You poke this little tool in and pull up to break the thread. It's sharp."

"Okay."

"Hold it like this."

"What is it?"

"Ripper. Seam ripper." Her voice faded as she returned to the sewing machine.

I concentrated my attention on the slender, pointy-tipped tool.

"Jack the Ripper," my mother muttered. Her stitches picked up speed.

∞

"Mama, can I have a sister?"

I was seven, pulling full-cut panties up over my navel and hopping on the cold morning floor.

My mother scrunched a leg of my beige leotards, creating a space for my toes to enter. "No, you cannot."

"A brother?"

"No."

"Why not?"

She held the leotard out, but I kept my foot glued to the floor. "I'm the only kid with no brothers or sisters. Tracy has five, plus her."

My mother blew air through her long nostrils.

"Nancy has six."

She shook the leotards at my feet.

I curled my toes under. "Rosemary has—"

My mother flung the leotards down. She marched out of the room and returned gripping something in her hand. Her face was triumphant, her voice smug. "This," she said, brandishing a plastic circle that rattled with small white pills, "this is why not."

I scrutinized the package. "What is it?"

"It's medicine for ladies who have plans for their lives."

There was something terrible about her explanation. I forced a smile to reassure us both. "You have a plan for being my mama. Right?" I lifted a foot and pointed it enticingly.

She dropped the package into the pocket of her apron. She quickly gathered up the leotard and unfurled half of it around my leg. Then she stood, leaving the rest to dangle between my thighs like a dejected tail.

"It's a big job being a mama, Marta. It's a big decision. Anyone who has five or six or eight children is trying to forget that. They forget what they've given up for it."

"Is the medicine for not forgetting, then?"

"Yes. It is. The medicine is for remembering all the other things." She crouched, smoothed the dropped leotard up my leg, and snapped the elastic around my waist.

"Pick a dress," she said.

Two were on my bed. I'd helped to sew the first: a knee-length jumper of green-and-white polyester plaid. My cozy white turtleneck lay under it. The other was a thigh-high orange coat dress with big striped buttons, sharp collar points, and a belt. My mother loved that dress. She'd hummed while she sewed it. She called it snazzy.

I picked the plaid. Mama turned and left my room. With her every step, I could hear the reminders jiggling in their pill case in her pocket.

∽

One strange still day I came home from third grade to find my mother leaning back in her sewing chair. Her eyes were almost closed. She held a cup of coffee in her lap. A blue wool garment rested under the machine's needle.

My gut tightened. "Mama? How come you're not making dinner?"

She turned. There was something different about her face: it was soft, like someone sleeping. She never looked like that. Her voice, too—soft. "Your father is going to be late tonight." Her words came to me as though she were somewhere else and someone else, not my mother at all.

She put her coffee on the table beside the portable sewing machine that was never in its carrying case. The room rang hollow without the background hiss of frying onions, without the sound of the machine.

"I'd like to finish this jacket before it gets too dark in here. Wash your hands. Have some bread and butter."

"Is there going to be dinner? Papa always—"

"I know what Papa wants."

"You can't. That's what he told me. You can't know what someone wants." I clutched my library book.

"He said that? How interesting. That's the first time I've heard of your father suggesting he might not know what's right for a person."

"He *can't* know. It's not his fault. No one knows for sure about anyone else. He said so."

My mother scrutinized me.

My blunt fingernails bit into my book's plasticized cover.

"Marta. People do change. Especially husbands and wives over the years. When your father and I met, I was just a child."

"You were kids?"

"Papa was older. He left our town to study in Canada. Everyone knew of him. He was going to be important."

"So you married him?"

"Not then."

"When?"

"Later, when he was already a dentist. He came back to visit his family, my neighbours. By that time I was almost eighteen."

"And you fell in love."

She looked at her lean stockinged feet. "Our town in Germany was so quiet. All I could think about was coming here with your father."

"And having me?"

She pointed her toes and her calves fisted up. "He tried to dissuade me. He said I wouldn't like it here. He said it was loud, unsettling, and the students behaved badly. It sounded just like the pictures I'd seen."

"What pictures?"

"My mother called him Herr Kanada—that was Papa to us. She told him I was quiet, strong, and serious, and would make a good wife."

"And then you got married."

She didn't answer. She didn't move.

"Mama?" I swayed a little to get her attention. "Was it really noisy when you came here?"

My mother's outstretched feet rocked from side to side. "No, Marta. Kingston was even quieter then than it is now. In the States, things were happening." She paused for a moment, her eyes unblinking. "But then it was too late." She shook her head slightly. "I thought I'd be playing a bongo with my baby on my back. But I was tired."

"Papa doesn't like loud things."

"Yes, Marta, I know."

"He says you don't have to be loud to make your point."

"Yes, he does."

"That's why he loves you, right? Because you're quiet and strong and . . . something."

She pursed her lips together hard, ringing them in white. Her lids shuttered her eyes. "Maybe. Maybe strong. And something." Her hands lifted to the wool, her body turning toward the machine.

I exhaled carefully and slipped into the kitchen to make my snack. Then I wandered over to her. Bread in one hand, I reached to stroke the blue-sheened fabric.

"Marta!" my mother snapped. "Get your fingers *off!*"

Her glare was fierce. She was back.

∞

On Saturdays my mother sewed for our family. She might remove my father's shirt collar and turn it over, replacing the frayed fabric with the fresh, brighter cotton that for years had been the collar's underside.

She might sew herself another respectable wife-of-dentist skirt, then stand at the mirror hitching the fabric higher, pulling it high above her knees to where her secret thighs touched.

She might sew me a dress, or a skirt, or a pair of pants. A crinkling vinyl midi dress, a fake fur skirt, a pair of flared white pants with perfect circles cut out near the ankles. All of these things, she did sew.

"'Use'? Christ almighty, Marta! There is no *use* for the cut-out. Are you eight or are you eighty?"

"It's not because I don't like it. It's just . . ."

"That's the part that takes it above everything else! The negative detail. That's what makes it stand out. The geometry. The finishing. That's *couture*. Look."

I looked, then looked away. I had thought these pants were going to be okay. I had been fitted for plain white pants; I'd held hope in my breath as my mother pulled pins from between her dry lips and adjusted the seams down the sides of my legs.

She yanked me back. "I said *look*. Do you see what it takes? It looks like a simple hole, but the workmanship, the skill you need to do this . . ."

"It's nice."

"*Pfah.*"

"Mama, the pants are nice. It's just . . ."

"You like them but you hate the only thing there is to like about them! Without the cut-out, they're nothing." She stretched a pant leg in her hands and held it between us.

I could see only the bar of white fabric and my mother's eyes. The empty circle twisted across her face where her mouth should have been.

"We don't have money to throw away," she said, "and I don't have time to keep making you things you never wear."

I looked down. I was in a pair of thin, comfortable, cotton-knit pants with an elastic waist—my favourites. "You made me these," I said softly.

"Those. Those you wear every day. What else have I made you? How many things have I made you with my own hands?"

"Lots."

"Pardon? 'Lots'?" Her hair whipped across her forehead like a dozen slashing eyebrows. "Good. Then you'll have more than enough to get by on."

3

ON SUNDAYS my father drove my mother and me to church. He waited outside, doing crossword puzzles in the car. After church he sat in his suit in the living room with dusty sunshine falling around him and watched wrestling.

His face lacked intensity of expression, so softly was it formed, but I could read his hands. He clenched them as the colour images came into view. He rose to turn the rabbit-ears on top. Then he settled, unsettled, into his usual chair. I would enter the living room, roll my eyes, then grasp the knob for colour balance and turn it to black-and-white.

The tension would deflate out of him then. He would collapse gratefully deep into his chair, his eyes on the TV, his lips releasing "My Marta" once, then murmuring silently on.

Papa's face was sketched in washes of subtle hues that would pale further as the years passed. His face did not crack or cry, but melted emotion into itself, dissipating it below the surface. His face was beige and soft, moulded into soft mounds over wide, flat cheekbones and a wide, soft jaw, but it gelled into focus above his suit.

His eyes seemed deeper when he put on the dark-grey summer wool jacket. Navy pinstripes ran down the suit, enclosing him in parallel lines. His large hands smoothed them, then rested, forgotten, on his ribs.

Papa had his story, the Old Leonard story. The years I was seven, eight, and nine, it lived with us like an odd hidden child, like a sibling I'd never really understand.

And then suddenly Papa and I together had a story. Our own story. It went like this: long-stifled mother leaves father and child.

At nine years old I didn't have a name for my mother's need, but I knew its shape within my chest.

There were times when she would turn from her sewing machine and see me watching her. She watched me watch her. She would sometimes try to give me a smile. But I waited, and always she turned back, back to her sewing, back to her thoughts. I would stand just long enough to be sure. Of what, I didn't know. But I knew that she turned back, and that I became a thing behind her once again. Like the teak sideboard with the pulled-glass ashtray balanced on it. Like the bumpy cardboard print of *Blue Boy* in its ornate frame. Like all the things that crowded up behind her, that pushed her closer to the machine, ever closer to the wall she faced.

I watched her head tilt down. I watched her elbows tuck in against her sides.

∽

Just before she left, my mother sewed new curtains for our dining room. I didn't see them until she stood on a chair hanging them. They were black and white, in a pattern that zigzagged like the line of a heart monitor or a lie detector, and had a row of black fringe at the bottom.

She hadn't let me help, though I was already sewing clothes with confidence, clothes I was not embarrassed to wear to grade four.

I sat frowning. "They're okay. I'm used to the old ones."

My mother said nothing.

"I could've sewn them, you know. I could've done it easily. You're always on the machine when I want to make something."

She was silent.

My father came in. "Let me hang those," he said. His voice quavered.

My mother ignored him, continuing to stretch up and to the right, reaching the swaying end of the loaded curtain rod toward the bracket screwed into the window frame. Her pantyhose pulled taut behind her knees.

My father shuffled out.

When she had hit the mark, my mother climbed down. She wiped her hands on her dress, and with her blue crocheted slippers she nudged the pile of fabric at her feet, the sprawling mound of our old curtains.

"My wedding gift from my mother," she said. "She sent me off to Canada with a trunk full of curtains. As soon as I got here, I threw them away."

"You threw away good curtains?"

"That's exactly what your father said ten years ago. I told him I could buy fabric here, modern and bright. He said, 'Buy with what? My old textbooks?' He said, 'Bring them back inside. Wash them and I'll hang them. Such good German lace.'" My mother laughed.

I pinched my bottom lip.

"Good German lace," she repeated, gathering the collection in her arms.

I heard her open the back door, then the screen door, then the stubborn lid of our metal garbage can.

∽

She woke me up to tell me. "I'm going now, Marta. You will hear from me. I've discussed it with your father. It will be you and him now, until you're ready to go, too."

She sat with perfect posture on the side of my bed, her face turned away from me, speaking toward the door. Then she kissed my forehead and left my room.

She hitchhiked to the border and worked her way south. She travelled with her box of threads, her blood-child swept aside like selvage.

∽

My father fell silent.

In the dining room the sewing machine waited. Home from school with a key around my neck, I walked carefully to my parents' room and stared at their empty, tidy bed, at the clear tops of dressers. I crept to her drawers and pulled them open. Her clothing waited. Her slips. Didn't she need slips where she was going? And panties. Silk scarves, sweet-smelling, the edges turned and sewn by hand, by her hand. Pantyhose coiled, balled like fists. Bras empty.

Emptiness settled on everything.

I walked through rooms examining the objects in our house. There was nothing here to bring my mother back. If she returned, it would not be for things. It would be for a life, a life better than the one she would find with her thumb out. If there could be a new life in our home. If I could make one.

If I wanted to make one. If I wanted her to return.

When my father came home each evening, he sat in the dining room: not hungry, not talking.

I chopped onions, slicing slowly with half-clenched eyes, the side of the blade stroking my knuckle. I sautéed mushrooms, watched their waters seep into the oil. I cooked, put pots and frying pans on the table, and sat across from my father, who nodded: thanks.

I could have run from the spark of panic in my gut, hid from the sight of my shaken father, but in those early days his silence held me. Suspended in the wordlessness of our home, drawing vegetables under a knife, I constructed order. Manning the gas stove, I controlled my own smouldering flame.

I cooked breakfast, then pressed the morning paper into my father's hands, lifting my face to smile encouragement into his eyes.

Whispered, hopeful songs wended through my body. I could defuse the message of my mother's flight, protect my father from her disdain. I would show him how to live on. I had only to continue, a stubborn, sensible girl-child. Jittery, with a tight grin, I bobbed to silent music as I watched my father from the corners of my eyes. I served porridge and sausages while he stared at nothing over the newspaper.

So I cooked. I cleaned. I coaxed Papa into each day. I held his hand on the way to school. I chatted to teachers and leapt into friendships, my breath tight. At night I sank into books, a reward for a good day's work.

∾

It was a few weeks after my mother left. My routines with my father were taking shape; our habits were helping him along. Weekday mornings were for walking to school.

It was a weekday: a school holiday Monday. I weighed the options, and said nothing.

My father walked me past the post office, past the parking lot and to within view of our church. He made a left and a quick right, and took me four paces into the schoolyard, which was normally scattered with children.

I felt my father hesitate. But I let go of his hand and strode toward the school, leaving him no choice but to turn and walk away. There was no one to ask if it should be otherwise, and how could he ask? He had not yet emerged from his silence and still looked to me for guidance.

I walked to the doors, which I knew would be bolted, and my father set off without me.

Hands behind my back, back against the cool metal doors, I rubbed my fingertips against the scratched blue paint—one raised heel pulsing rhythmically, my stiff shoulders slowly moving forward and back—until my father disappeared around the corner. Exhaling, I slid down. I felt the seams of my leotards pressing into the flesh of my buttocks and the waistband gaping low at the back. Cool springtime air slipped up my spine. The concrete was hard and rough on my palms.

I picked up the front of my dress. Between my legs, a taut arc of beige leotard spanned my lower thighs, bisected by a loopy seam that rolled up to my belly button.

Leotards were a wonder to me as a child, a kind of magic that gave you grown-up legs. On school days the magic could be broken by the sight of a single confident ten-year-old in bright white knee socks, but not on that alone day. That day I yanked up my leotards, compacting my toes and stretching the waist higher, then stood and surveyed the terrain.

Emptied of the usual clusters of children, the schoolyard was stripped, too, of its anguish points. The parking blocks were mine to walk on—and I did, balancing all the way to the ends, where rusty reinforcing rods jutted from the crumbling cement. There was no one to hear me chant in the spaces between the balance beams. No one to chase me from her territory. No boys to grab shark-like at my chubby legs or to flip up the back of my dress. At the end of the line I ran to the basketball net, dribbling frantically, and flipped an imaginary ball through its naked rim. Then I kept running, all the way to the muddy grass where the older kids usually slumped and snorted, laughed and flirted, and spread rumours about my father.

I ran with determination and purpose, grinding the young blades of grass into the sloppy earth. A thief, a traitor to convention, I crossed the muddy expanse time and again, claiming it, cleansing it, annihilating its history.

The clouds had already wet my face with feeble strands of spit. Now they pelted streams of rain that washed the mud from my shoes and dripped off my nose. I stood four paces in from the high schoolyard fence.

Papa returned. His stride was fast, fearful, and determined. His hand was out; I waited for it.

"It's raining," he said. It was an accusation and an awaken-
ing. It was spoken in quiet wonder, addressed to everything.

My mother was gone, and my father had spoken.

I took his hand.

I took the credit with the blame.

∞

Bit by bit my father found words, quiet, soothing words.

"Marta," he said, pausing as he followed me out the door
one morning, "it's all right."

"That's good, Papa." I blinked back quick tears. His small
voice alarmed me more than his silence ever had.

"We'll be fine, Marta."

"Of course."

"We just have to keep on. Go forward. We have to sell the
house."

"Okay." I took his hand but turned my face away, my
surprised smile, my sudden pride. I had done it: We were
moving, leaving this house behind, leaving my mother's scent,
escaping.

I began packing that night, folding my mother's clothing
into cardboard boxes, taping them shut, and pushing them
from my mind.

In the corner of the dining room, next to the sewing table,
stood the rippled plastic case for her machine. In all my years
I'd never seen its insides. Now I cracked it open. Its inner walls
were as smooth, precise, and hollow as an empty chest cavity,
with gently sloping protrusions shaped to support and protect.

I stood up quickly. For a moment my mind throbbed with
the sound of my mother's sewing. Then I shot out a hand and

yanked the machine's power cord from the wall. Still dizzy and with trembling arms, I pulled the heavy sewing machine to my torso and lowered it down the length of my body. It fell awkwardly into its case. I stuffed in the cords and found a place for the foot pedal, then I drew the sides of the shell together and snapped the lock.

My heart grew suddenly calm. The flash of panic was contained. If I could not extinguish it, I could at least confine it.

I vowed to never release my mother's sewing machine from its case.

4

IN THIS, OUR NEW STORY, my father painted. Through that summer and autumn he rose in the morning and shaved, then ate what I laid on the table and left our apartment in his pinstriped suit. He carried clean coveralls in a bag on his arm.

He painted carefully. People said he was the best house painter in all of Kingston. They loved the dash of accent in his quiet English. They loved his way with Victorian trim. They loved the glimpse of knotted tie at the throat of his coveralls. They thought him quaint—"that quiet little man"—with just the right hint of scandal.

His brushes were soft and supple, fresh from their Varsol bath. His face was smooth, but his hands shook. They trembled on the arms of his chair in the living room, on the stems of his fork and knife. They trembled as he worked a screwdriver in under the lid of a can of paint. Yet his line was straight, the bristles calm, the wet surface serene, when his hand with the brush stroked the wood.

My father painted entire houses, inside and out, after he left dentistry. After dentistry left him.

I knew what people said. I'd heard it in the schoolyard. That he'd drilled through Old Leonard's eye. That he'd entered the brain. That he'd done experiments, German experiments. People liked those stories.

My father watched wrestling.

"Is it Sweet Mauler Brown?" I asked, and he took my hand and smiled.

Ladies called in the early morning. I answered the phone and they talked to me.

"Tell your father there's an extra something for him if he starts before Thursday."

"Let your dad know the furniture's coming early. He'll have to finish up this weekend."

"Tell him that James is pleased but I'm having second thoughts about the colour."

"Have your father drop by at lunchtime. Tell him I'm thinking maroon."

My father ate oatmeal. I slipped messages into his thoughts and straightened his tie. I prepared him to leave our home each morning, fortifying him with a strong look, weighing down his bag with a stash of sandwiches, the bread cut thick and rough as love.

I turned ten that September. Still my father held my hand as we walked, and he counted the blocks to school. He counted quietly. Though he had long since given up silence, his numbers were at times his only words.

"One. Two."

I could feel his hesitation as we turned the corner. Was it a new block or only a trick, this skew of the linear? My father believed in forward.

The turn merited a skipped breath, then a quick "Three," after which he increased his pace.

He counted through the short autumn and into the early winter. One cold day I simply stopped. I wanted words. Round words, whole words, words with heft and feeling. Not numbers that bounced off my skull like the brick-red rubber balls in gym.

At "Three," my hand had been in my father's, my footsteps had flown beside his, all was the way it had been.

Then all wasn't enough.

My father's gloved hand slid cleanly off my own. The hem of his coat shifted briskly on his shins, leapt with every step of his boots.

I stood and watched him striding away from me, my fingers lifted to the horizon. I stood, still and pointing, while my father continued on.

∽

My mother's clothing was gone, gone in boxes to the Salvation Army and now residing on other women's skin. Her jewellery was a mystery. It had disappeared while I packed for our move, surely taken by my father, but I saw reminders of it, of her, for years.

Tiny intrusions interrupted my days. The aquamarine of my grade six teacher's pendant made me avert my eyes. The turquoise ring a boy gave me in grade seven got stuffed into a drawer. While my girlfriends stitched beads and sequins to their collars, I scribbled on my sneakers in pen.

When grade eight graduation loomed, my father lifted my hand in his. "You should have something special," he said. He gently gripped my ring finger, measuring with touch and eyes.

"A book would be great," I said, pulling my hand away.

"Anything but jewellery, please. I can't see myself wearing a ring."

∾

I see myself in early high school: a pressed uniform hanging like a bell from strong shoulders, my body a plump worm under the scratchy wool. Running in navy gym bloomers: ankles and knees, elbows and pointy girl-breasts jumping. Perching hesitantly in the doorway of our walk-up apartment. With a step, entering a custard of routine and protection—the pablum of loving care I bestowed upon my father within our new home.

The money from the sale of our house had run out. In the winter Papa worked marking student papers for a correspondence school that offered certificates in 150 interests. He was paid by the page.

In those long, cold days I would return home to find him pacing in our small living room with a stack of exams or essays spread across the coffee table, or sitting fretting over papers with the end of his pencil between his teeth. When I walked in, his eyes darted to me in appeal.

He couldn't bring himself to pass or fail people. He didn't even know them. How could he judge them? They were not offered a chance to speak in their defence.

Once, coming home to find him anxious on the sofa, I approached quietly and sat beside him. I was fourteen and had grown uncomfortable hugging him, but I put an arm around his shoulders and he leaned into it.

"Just try, Papa."

He turned to look at my murmuring smile.

"You don't have to be perfect and neither do they. Give them some slack. Everyone deserves a break."

He sucked in his lip and held out his arm. His hand with the sharpened pencil hovered over a page.

I waited.

Finally I got up and walked to the kitchen. I glanced back, but he had not moved, save for the intense shaking of the pencil in the air.

"Papa," I snapped, "no one cares if they get a B-minus or a C-plus. All anyone wants is to pass and get out."

All the grade ten girls at my school took Home Economics. It was an elective, an easy credit: cook and eat, make a budget, plan a month of balanced meals.

And sew.

The guidance counsellor was incredulous. "You don't want Home Ec?"

"I don't sew."

"Well, exactly. It's a valuable household skill. One day, when you have children—"

"I won't sew," I said. "I don't and I won't."

With my friends I threw hoops in the school gym and bruised my forearms with volleyballs. We slurped cut oranges during games and untangled our slender necklaces in change rooms afterwards. We talked of lay-ups and saves, of necking and hickeys.

Some days we had late practices or played against other schools. I planned ahead, leaving long, tidy notes for my father to direct him through the warming of his dinner.

I kept my home life to myself. When my friends whined about chores—"I had to clean out the hairbrush!"—I moaned with them. I didn't criticize their messy bedrooms and didn't envy them either. The bond I had with my home, I cherished. I'd worked on it, worked for it, had made it mine. My neat, sparse room and the hushed public library were my favourite places. They were my escape, my respite. Everywhere else was an adventure, large and invigorating, exciting and uncertain.

When I turned sixteen, I celebrated: almost an adult. I made a chocolate birthday cake from a mix, a special treat, and prepared a meal I loved—beef stew with dumplings—which my father loved, too. Papa came home at the end of the day and actually started singing.

Slapping slippers in his hands, he kept time to an unfamiliar German song. It was upbeat and seemed romantic, perhaps amorous. He made me laugh.

He'd brought home beer, a rarity, a six-pack of IPA. I found the opener and we drank with dinner. It wasn't my first taste of beer, but it was the first time I'd had more than half a bottle to myself. Papa opened one at a time and topped up our glasses as though we were drinking wine.

"So my little girl is sixteen."

"Finally."

"What's the hurry? Everything will happen in its own time."

"Sixteen is much better than fifteen."

"No age is better," he replied. "You'll see. Different, yes, especially when you're young. But better? I don't think so."

"Well, I do. I know so."

He said nothing.

I took a drink of beer. "Do you even remember when I was little? Or you think that was as good as now?"

"There's no point comparing. Life is really just one day, the day you're in. Overnight you trade it for the next day."

"And so on."

"That's right."

"Like a car." My glass was empty again. I held it out for a refill.

"Like a car," Papa agreed. "Except every morning you have a clean odometer. Presto, ready to go."

"A car with no reverse."

"What's your point, Marta?"

"Nothing. It's fine. You're right, Papa." My nose was runny. My eyes watered, too.

"You're not getting a cold? Because if you're getting a cold . . ."

What would he do for me? He didn't finish. He didn't know.

"It's the beer," I said and hiccupped. "It's the hiccups." We both laughed.

After dinner, leaning back in his chair, my father belched and looked shocked, and I laughed again. I lifted my beer glass and drank lustily, happy with the wet glass in my hands.

Papa grew pensive. He gestured toward my face, his fingers and his gaze loose in the air. "You look like your mother when I met her."

My jaw tightened. "Have more cake."

"Something about your eyes."

I picked up the knife.

He looked away, looked at the curtains. "Sixteen. If you're anything like your mama, you'll be—"

"I'm cutting. This big? Or bigger? Pass your plate." I heaped it, a small piece on top of a big piece, a candle stuck in the top. "There. Now we can sing again. Now you make a wish, Papa! Your cake is getting waxy."

My father blew and I plucked out the smoking candle.

"Ah, Marta. I wish—"

"Don't tell! You can't say it out loud; it won't come true. You need a new fork." And I ran from the table to fetch one.

That night I tucked myself in, rolling gently from side to side until I lay safe and contained in my tube of blankets.

I was sixteen. Our home was in careful order; my father was getting by; my friendships and school life shone with subtle teenage rebellion. I was doing everything right, just right. Anyone would think so.

I'd created the perfect picture of freedom and love—and without having to pack up and leave.

I closed my eyes. Immediately my head plummeted, dropping me upside down. The bed spun.

I bolted up and ran to the bathroom. Clutching my pillow, I settled on the floor against the bathtub, hoping Papa wouldn't wake to relieve himself.

The next morning was clear, and I felt empty and slow. I washed the dinner dishes, rinsed the six beer bottles, and let my father sleep in.

When I came home from school, there was a small white box on the table where I'd left his lunch bag. Inside, on a bed of white sponge on a grey card with "Regal Jewellery" stamped in silver, was a pair of screw-on earrings. They were golden with sky-blue beads, one bead to sit against the lobe, the other to dangle below it.

My ears were pierced; I wore nothing but plain gold keepers. That was okay; I didn't expect my father to notice. My mother had worn clip-ons. It was all he would have known.

Under the box was a note: *"I forgot to give you your present last night. Happy birthday, my young lady. Happy birthday, Marta. Don't grow up too fast. Love, Papa."*

Just one year later: clutching at womanhood. Lungs burning with desperate breath. Wet thighs clenching, yearning to grip my young lover's hands, legs. Slippery smooth head of penis, startling shaft—in it all went. Out, and I wobbled home, mind clear as the summer sky, belly sticky as glue.

It was not Kurt who rode me that first time in the dry grass beyond the stadium. He was unknown to me then, a young man in Halifax, unknowable. He did not watch me slim down and accept the forces of gravity. He did not see me finish high school, nor glimpse my graduation photo. It glinted in our living room, showed me eyeing the camera with amusement, a young woman inured to anxiety. Not so much curious as open. Inviting—daring—all stimuli.

Kurt came later.

5

AT TWENTY-SIX I CAME TO TORONTO. I rode the subway train hurtling eastbound. The tunnel walls dropped away and sharp, springtime sunlight slashed in. Bridge girders flew by, black slaps on the cool light. I felt I was sprinting past the bars of a jail cell. Below, a swath of forest sandwiched a smear of river and a snaking highway. Then the train re-entered its underground burrow, and I wondered: *Where am I?*

Above the doors was a subway map. Next stop, Broadview.

That would do.

St. Boniface Church was simply there when I exited the station. It is what brought me here: first to Patsy Wallace, then to Mrs. Oland.

Tall and white, almost unadorned, its limestone walls stained by weeping eavestroughs, the church had a benignly accepting look about it. Not so much *Enter and find refuge,* as *Do with me what you will.*

"All right," I muttered. "I'll take a shot."

Behind the church, on a small, raised lawn, a century home was marked "Rectory Hours: 10 to 4 Weekdays." It was Friday.

"Fish tonight," I said, raising my finger to the doorbell. The door was dark oak with bevelled glass windows.

I glanced through one of its panes and gasped. Hope stabbed up like a crocus.

Asha had left her doll there.

There is a way that love clings to our insides, not like raindrops but like burrs. It sticks and sticks, and when we pick at it, it sticks some more, in pieces smaller and smaller and harder to grasp.

A doll sat on an upholstered chair in the foyer. But Asha had not been there, not ever. *Asha will never.*

Another child's toy faced me, another plastic doll with matted yellow hair. A young stranger's forgotten doll, and above it, my face in a mirror, a stricken face in a silver frame.

I pushed out a cluster of breaths. I steadied my legs. I talked myself back to the threshold of whatever would become my future.

Then I pressed the doorbell, a chill in my hands and two creeping splashes of red on my cheeks, two islands of blood under tired, bloodshot eyes.

The bell was answered by a woman who looked not unlike me: wavy brown hair, a round face, slightly less than plump. She wore a tan vest and matching skirt and a short-sleeved ivory blouse. She was older than me. She may have been thirty-five, though her clothes aged her beyond that. She had a quick, shallow smile.

I realized with surprise that my lips were trembling.

"Hello," I said. "I would like to join your parish."

It was Patsy Wallace who ushered me into the rectory that Friday, eyeing my sweatpants and sagging duffle bag. She was quick with assessment, yet I could see the confusion in her eyes.

I knew that my face, though pale and shaken, had a measure of intelligence in its lines. I quickly dampened it, dropping my gaze and flooding my features with insecurity.

Patsy smiled.

In a small office near the front of the house, she gave me a form and motioned to a chair. She glanced toward the hall, her mouth twitching down at the sound of childish footsteps on the stairs to the second floor. A frown pinched two lines between her brown eyes.

"Make yourself comfortable. We'll start right here," she said, raising well-groomed brows. "It's just a wee questionnaire. Unless, that is, you'd like me to fill it out for you?" Eagerness nipped at her words. I could see that this was a woman who knew exactly what she wanted.

I slackened my jaw and pulled it in on itself to create the suggestion of a weak chin. "You would? I don't really . . . If you would. If that's okay."

Patsy glowed. "Name?" she asked brightly.

"Marta Fett. Spelled F-E-double T."

Her face dimmed. "I see. Well, then, address?"

I hesitated just long enough to perk her up again, and said, "I don't have an address of my own. Not yet. I just got here from . . . from Kingston. And Germany before that. I came here straight from the bus station, and I saw your church." Chin down, I locked eyes with her. "Something called me here."

Sins of omission, they say, but I've never noticed that in the Commandments.

Patsy drew a breath, her mouth spreading wide, and gazed at the form with tenderness. "Marta. What an unusual name.

Lovely, really. I know you must be a special person. You may, in fact, be just the thing we're looking for."

And so Patsy Wallace took me into the flock of St. Boniface. Not only was I registered as a new parishioner, I was given a room and a job.

"For a while, anyway. We'll see how it goes." Patsy seemed to want to withdraw the offer as soon as she'd made it. I think she might have, too, except that Father Jerome appeared and was introduced.

He was a slight man, neither young nor old, in a cardigan both too long and too tight, and dark grey trousers over white sneakers. His ears were almost startling, not only because they were noticeably perfect but also because his hair seemed cut to display them. His face was long and disproportionately lean, with a vertical cleft in each cheek. It was framed by dull brown hair, thin on top and straggling at the sideburns, trimmed short around the perfect ears and left to curl like a toddler boy's at the nape. His voice was unmanageable. It bumped against higher tones which he checked sharply, so that it seemed to swerve in and out of a respectable, masculine mid-range.

"You'll be helping us get this place into shape, Marta? Wonderful! All and any help is appreciated. I've been after Patsy for weeks to find a bright young woman. She got so used to being our number-one volunteer she still thinks she can do everything around here! But now she's our official, part-time *salaried* rectory administrator—aren't you, Patsy?—in addition to her ongoing volunteering and good deeds in the parish community . . . *heh heh*. And the back bedroom is fine for you, Marta—not too small? You haven't seen it? Well, come on, then! Patsy will be glad to . . ."

And so I began to work full-time at the rectory. I didn't stay long, however, just long enough to distinguish myself. Patsy shuttled me in and out of there even faster than she could reform a sinner.

For twelve days I addressed the surfaces and trappings of the rectory. I vacuumed, avoiding the front offices when Father Jerome sat with a parishioner or when Patsy leaned out, frowning, one hand holding the phone and the other waving at me. I swept city grime and assorted litter off the front porch. I washed dishes and dried them by hand. I even poked about the tiny front flower garden once. Under last year's fallen leaves, a cluster of pale, foolish shoots was reaching for the March sun.

No one asked me to watch Matthilda, Patsy's quiet, delicate four-year-old, but I flicked off the vacuum when I noticed her closing her eyes and ears to its drone; I took care not to crowd her out of the chosen corners to which she retreated with books or crayons after morning kindergarten; I didn't chase her feet with a mop or create a peak of soap suds on her nose.

She was not quick with a smile, and she didn't look for one from me. She had the run of the house, but seldom did she run. She eased along walls. She haunted the edges of windows, inhaling at the seams of wood, caulk, and glass. She drifted into corners.

I spoke one sentence to her: "I'm Marta and I'm here to clean." She didn't respond, but after that she stared longer, with the balance tipped in favour of curiosity, against fear.

No one asked me to be friendly, and I wasn't. I was Marta the maid. Good with a mop. Minds her own business.

The truth was a live-in maid was not needed there. The rectory's two floors—two office rooms flanking the front door, and two upstairs bedrooms, plus my little bedroom nook behind the kitchen—were easy to keep neat and clean once the accumulated dust was cleared away. Before my second week was up I was wondering what to do with myself. It was clear that either someone would have to come right out and ask me to nanny Matthilda, or I'd have to start paying rent.

Then unexpectedly I was saved from either possibility. I was chosen for this life with Mrs. Oland: perhaps for the rhythm of my mop, perhaps for the pasty gratitude with which I blunted my speech, perhaps for the little spouts of panic that sometimes ticked around my eyes.

"Marta, come here. Marta?" Patsy Wallace leaned out of her office, annoyance crimping the edges of her smile. "Wonderful news! Mrs. Oland, the old dear—you know? You saw her at Mass. She sits in the front left pew, walks with a cane? Mrs. Oland has agreed to give you a try."

"A try?"

"She needs some help with her things. She isn't long for this world, God bless her. Thank heaven she's finally decided to listen to my advice. It'll be the best thing for her, having someone stay with her."

Someone? Was I being evicted already, sent to live with that bone-thin old woman? To live close to her, to watch over her? I could feel the hairs on my arms slide up.

I imagined myself tiptoeing through Mrs. Oland's home, unprepared for encounter, unwilling to help the old woman hobble toward her afterlife.

I imagined myself watching her, afraid to blink as the seconds ticked by, one finger poised over the phone with the emergency number memorized.

I imagined her shrinking and shrivelling at my nervous touch.

"So, no reason to procrastinate. Shall we pop over now? You can bring your bag. It's only a few blocks away, and you might as well get settled in earlier than later."

"All right," I said. "So I'm done here? I'm fired?"

"Oh, Marta!" Patsy's laugh was a practised trill. She came close and placed her hands on my shoulders. Her face was a parody of empathy and love. I was amazed that I'd ever thought she looked like me. "You'll never be 'done here.' You're part of the family!"

She turned to pull her jacket from the back of her chair. "Come to clean on Wednesdays; that should do it. No point in wearing down the finish on the floors any sooner than we need to. If you only knew what it costs to varnish them."

It did not endear me to Mrs. Oland that she was crying when we arrived. Her narrow face sank into its tears as though her cheekbones were collapsing. That didn't bother me. The problem was her forehead, which was clenched into crevices of fury. When she first spoke, I thought she stuttered, but it was only the anger gripping her words.

"How c-could you, P-Patsy! How could you come to my home and f-force a stranger on me? I'm old but I'm not stupid. I still have a choice."

We followed her slow, cautious walk into the bungalow's carefully cluttered living room. The shelves and end tables held clusters of figurines, crystal, and display china. The room smelled old, of flat air tempered with wistfulness, of unreachable dust and the aging remnants of well-bred perfumes. Boxes poked out from under the upholstered chairs and the floral embroidered sofa, whose underside dangled long threads at one end. An arched opening led to the dining room, and another from there to the kitchen, where a boxy gold refrigerator clashed with 1950s grey-green cupboards and a white gas stove.

Patsy had her hand on my elbow, steering it, stopping it from doing her ribs harm. She sighed melodically, as though relieved to have all the tension finally out in the open, as though all bad feeling had been blown away by the sweet breath of Jesus.

"Now you'll feel better, Mrs. Oland. There you go. Have a seat, both of you, and why don't I put the kettle on. You'll be so happy with Marta."

As she walked toward the kitchen and Mrs. Oland and I sat down, she called back, "All these months I've been looking for just the right companion for you, just like you asked me to, and here our prayers have been answered."

Mrs. Oland didn't raise her pitch above that of the running water. "Prayers," she rasped. She put her fingertips together. I didn't think she was praying, but Patsy, poking her head out of the kitchen, smiled sweetly.

"Marta has been very helpful at the rectory. As I told you. And you do need someone to help with your project. As you told me." She looked about as though she might sit down, then caught herself. "So I'll be off! The everyday teacups are above the sink, Marta, in the cupboard to the right. I'll let Mrs. Oland tell you how she takes her tea: black, one sugar."

I stood and cleared my throat. Mrs. Oland looked startled. She wasn't crying any more. She wasn't angry. Patsy's presence filled the room, and even I could feel the impending vacuum that would accompany her exit. Mrs. Oland seemed almost to be trembling in anticipation of it. I sat down again to anchor us both.

"Your room is in the basement," Patsy said, moving toward the door. "Find the sheets, find whatever you need; there's a linen closet down there. Don't leave the kitchen cupboards open, Marta. And turn the pot handles in." She dropped her hand to her side and motioned impatiently for me to come near. I rose and went over with an apologetic glance at Mrs. Oland.

Patsy whispered. "You'll get the hang of it. It won't be for long."

She scooted back in to kiss Mrs. Oland on the cheek.

"The tea, Marta!"

Then she was gone.

6

MRS. OLAND HAS FASCINATING TEETH, long and thin, crammed together so that one turns this way, the other faces it, a third holds stubbornly to a forward position unaltered in almost nine decades. Her teeth are yellow, silver, and grey. The white has been scrubbed away. I discourage Mrs. Oland from smearing her lips with colour. The natural pale purple of her mouth, the narrow band of lips, sets off to perfection the elegant tones of her teeth, the metallic tints, the dabs of gold.

When I first moved in, I knew only the cutting edges of those teeth. I heard the work of the stubborn ridges as she chewed. I did not attempt to cajole Mrs. Oland into a smile. Nevertheless she soon came to show the full glory of her teeth as she talked, drawing back her lips ever more frequently, tentative smiles sliding into chuckles as she leaked her intentions to my ears.

"You have lovely teeth," I told her.

She gathered her lips over them. "I'm afraid I can't manage flossing any more." We both looked at her hands.

I floss her teeth.

In the morning she brushes while I drink coffee at the dining room table. I place my cup on the white table pad, thinking once again that we should conceal it with a suitable cloth. Mrs. Oland joins me. Sitting forward, her bones depressing the patterned velvet seat, her elbows cocked and wrists jutting, she grips the table. Her mouth is open, rigid like a baby bird's, like a scream. I wind the floss around my fingertips and slide it back and forth in the tight, dark slits between the slender teeth. My eyes squint against the old, minty breath. I exhale seldom and carefully, conscious of the warm wet odour of coffee directed at Mrs. Oland's scrawny throat.

Everything about her is thin. Her nose has little leeway for tapering. It begins thin and ends abruptly.

("My nose is going to be even pointier than yours," Asha said years ago. "It's going to be as pointy as a carrot"— drawing her fingers before it, pinching them together a foot from its rounded tip. I want to do the same for Mrs. Oland: coax a pointy tip for that stunted protuberance.)

"Close," I say finally. It takes her a few moments to bring her face to life. When the jaw clamps shut, her face looks bruised and vulnerable. I stroke her cheek lightly. "Good, Mrs. Oland. Another morning done."

I was brought here for this: to pack, to floss, to be very careful with everything.

I have a room in Mrs. Oland's bungalow, two small lawns to water and weed, cans of soup to open and heat. My appetite has adjusted to Mrs. Oland's, and we don't eat much. They pay me at the church for my weekly tidy-up—not a lot, but I don't need a lot, and now I can eat soup for dinner without my stomach grumbling.

∞

The first two Wednesdays at the rectory go smoothly: Patsy gives me directions and I follow them. I don't mind if she considers me a tool. Tools, I think, have their own dignity. This is why we bond with them. I am inclined to respect them.

My yellow-gloved arms are in the oven when Patsy's little girl enters the kitchen with her hands behind her back. It's not my duty to feed her, but as I squat on my haunches and watch her shuffle sideways to the fridge, I can't help using the long-unused words.

"Are you hungry?"

She shakes her head. Her hands fidget behind her, feeling for the handle of the fridge door.

"Would you like me to make you a sandwich?"

Her eyebrows scrunch down as she wraps her fingers around the door handle. She takes a deep breath. What a little thing she is, small for her age. Her shoulders are narrow and almost pointy, could use some meat on them, could use my hands around them, could nest like eggs in my palms.

She pulls the door open and stumbles forward a step. Then, quick as a whisper, she pivots, thrusts her arm into the fridge and brings out a bright green apple.

Behind her it goes. Both hands hold it against the small of her back as she scurries away down the hall.

I hear the front door open and a man's voice.

"Morning, Mrs. Wallace, or maybe afternoon. Well, waltzing Matthilda, what do you got there?"

"For you, Harold." I hear her smile. "I got it for you myself."

∞

That evening Mrs. Oland sits me down and telephones her beloveds. This is what she says to each: "My dear, there's nothing to concern yourself with. My only hope is that I'm able to finish putting my affairs in order . . . The paintings, the stocks and bonds . . . One must be so careful in deciding who will get what. There's a girl in now who helps me. I've given her the basement flat.

"But she's not a stranger! She has a job at the church. German. Very quiet. Keeps to herself. You know how they are: serious. Very careful with everything."

When she completes her round of phone calls, her high cheeks are pink and clear. Dead or alive, she will alter the beloveds' sense of the past, or steer them toward what might still be possible, through the influence of her collected minutiae. The stocks, the paintings—it hardly matters that they do not exist; they can still stir yearnings and regrets. Like the vases and dishes, the commemorative teaspoons and miniature sugar bowls, they can still inspire dreams or a sense of loss.

I do not dishearten her. For what else are owned objects if not the touchstones and containers of our histories and our hopes? Could the beloveds resist the crisp, aged vapour of those imaginary stock certificates, the promise of an untarnished family reputation sloshing from an heirloom teapot, the expectation of a better future displayed as a silk brocade cushion? Could they hang up the phone and continue on, unchanged and unrepentant? Open their parcel and fail to ask themselves why they received this and not that?

Would Mrs. Oland's granddaughter still host casual barbe-
cues knowing that her proof of lineage would rest unflaunted
in her hall closet: handwoven Irish linens too precious to
expose to yellow mustard? Would not the first gathering
worthy of a fine linen tablecloth begin a process of insidious
yearning for a more elegant life?

The beloveds are vulnerable. Their history makes them so:
a history shaped by objects. I know this. Mrs. Oland tells me
again every time she turns and says something like, "To whom
shall this go? It was given to me by Pierre and sat on the piano
when the children were young."

Or muses: "I promised this to Arthur, but he promised he
would phone me, and I haven't heard from him since
Christmas."

Or: "Laura has the salt shaker; I've threatened to give the
pepper mill to Kimberly."

She tells me all this with a lilting serenity, for in well-
intentioned revenge she has found her mission and her way, a
way to be more meaningfully generous. In this I am her servant.

I am the cold, quiet assistant, the infiltrator come to take
advantage of Mrs. Oland in her final days: So they think, the
parishioners and friends, the daughters and sons. Their
thoughts are in their voices when I answer the phone and in
Mrs. Oland's words when she hangs up and looks me over.

"They'll get used to you, Marta. Don't mind the nasty
things they say."

I have seen their names on packages. I know them by their
possessions, wrapped, boxed, and stamped, but as yet undeliv-
ered. I know that Mr. Aitkins will get the silver creamer—but
not the sugar bowl, because he once chastised Mrs. Oland for

sweetening her tea. A granddaughter, Olivia, will have pearls for purity. Mrs. Oland's daughter Yolanda: figurines, stationery, numerous things. Lena, Susan, Chester . . . There are many beloveds. They are all recorded, all entrusted with objects.

Only I remain unlabelled, unaccounted for. Ms. Marta Fett does not appear on the addressed parcels in the hallway beside the linen closet. I do not receive mail.

Yet I do know people, in a way. I chat. I ask, as if truly curious, "What does your husband do for a living? Your child is how old?" at afternoon social gatherings to which I am occasionally invited through the mutual agreement of all the guests, all looking out for Mrs. Oland's best interests.

I speak to Patsy: "You're lucky you can bring Matthilda to work with you. I guess you're glad she's such a quiet, easy child."

And to Father Jerome: "Any laundry today? Wash or dry clean? Your sermon on Sunday was lovely, uplifting," as I move in and out of his stifling room, heading to the basement when I cannot bear chatting any longer.

To the mailman, I smile each day, palm up. Letters should not clatter around in a metal box. They should be delivered to a human hand, even if it must be mine.

7

THERE ARE LETTERS in this story. There are always letters.

I was nineteen in late springtime in Kingston. The downtown was sprinkled with tourists expecting the revered writer Robertson Davies to stroll from between the limestone edifices, or harried escaped convicts to spring from behind the bushel baskets in the outdoor market, like Pip's benefactor from behind a tombstone. The lower ground was often swathed in early morning fog from the lake, moisture I breathed in and coddled as I entered my workplace.

There had been no money for university after high school, and so instead I worked in a bakery. By six-thirty its picture windows were steamy, as if some great hand had captured the dawn in our glass box and cranked up the temperature to Roast.

I foiled those godly preparations daily. As the assistant to the baker, I provided a second set of eyes in the early morning: enough security to permit the propping open of the front door. I came in and the heat and steam rushed out, propelling into the front room the baker, who adored me.

"Good morning, Fräulein!" he roared as he approached.

"Morning, Zach," I muttered, reaching for a broom.

It was emotional shift work. Zach was brilliantly happy in the mornings. I was quiet, irritable, and withdrawn. By nine his joy would fade and my sunny side would begin to rise; I would inhale the aroma of egg bread and warm cinnamon rolls, and pluck pinches of dough for my salivating mouth. It was a partnership of equals, though Zach was close to sixty and I was little more than a teenaged sales clerk.

I smacked the toes of his flour-whitened shoes with the broom. "Get back there and work."

He smiled as though I had kissed him. "My lovely Fräulein, you are cruel this morning!" He twittered then disappeared.

I leaned against the smooth slant of a display case and gazed for a long time out the open front door. The mist was gone. The day had begun.

It would be a long one.

∞

When I returned home, there was a letter on my bed. Is it possible I recognized my mother's handwriting at a distance of three intrepid steps and ten lived years?

And the date at the top: that day.

I stood at my bedroom door and stared. Then I turned and retraced my path down the hall.

I made dinner, still in my dusty work clothes.

The apartment door opened. My father stepped into the bouquet of fried onions—always it was onions, the rich smell of coming home.

His quiet was devoid of its usual fullness. He left his coveralls in their bag on the hallway floor and washed up in the bathroom. He sat at the table without looking at me. He touched his cutlery and placed his disquieted hands in his lap.

I waited.

Between us sat oval bowls of mashed potatoes and fried onions, circles of carrots, and slices of cold meat. I watched my father's eyes search for my expression in the ribbon of fat at the edges of the beef, in the rippled hills of potatoes, in the contours of his cotton napkin, which wrinkled along the shrunken thread of its hem.

A day earlier I would have scanned his face with love and concern, let him sense my love as comforting and welcome as the forkfuls of familiar food. I would have smiled contentedly into my plate, feeling his silence like an understood hug all around me. A day earlier he would have sat with his hands trembling slightly, but of no concern, in his lap, with his head raised to mine, his eyes lingering half-focused on my chin or my ear.

He would not have been wondering what I was thinking. He would not have been scared of me, nor for me, nor of what he had done.

"So?" I said.

He looked at me, right at me, right into my eyes. "I promised I would give it to you. She—well, we—thought . . ." His voice broke.

"I don't want to know." I crossed my legs and arms.

"It's been ten years, Marta. It's ten years today."

It should have been a day like any other; it had to be. My mouth was dry and full; a balloon was closing against my throat. I forced my lips to stretch around it.

"I know," I said.

"And we thought that this way you'd be old enough to understand—"

"The letter's been here all this time?"

"Yes."

"You've had it here, in our home, for ten years?"

His eyes widened. "I promised."

"Ten years of hiding what was mine to know!"

I could have walked into those unguarded eyes as though they were open doors. His lips, too, hung open and mute.

"And she?" The words spat out. Had I ever so much as said "she" of my mother in the decade past? Ever mentioned her at all, ever thought of her without sweeping the thought away like contaminated flour? "What did *she* promise you?"

His eyes looked into mine, the pupils pulsing once. I had to glance away from him, from those unfamiliar, bare eyes.

He said, "The postcard, of course. She promised to send the postcard."

My chin snapped up. "What postcard?"

"On your bed, with the letter. The postcard came in today's mail."

The letter. My mother's epitaph, left behind when she crossed to the other side. A note to tack up against the backdrop of her freedom.

Dear Marta,

    I write to you as you will be when you read this: no longer a young girl but a young woman. You were always a perceptive child. You always knew I needed more—more life

than could be lived in our home. I could see in your eyes that
you knew I would leave.

I could see that I should.

The best thing I could give you—what I am giving you
today—is the picture of courage and purpose I create for you
with my departure. Always be willing to sacrifice in order to
achieve your dreams, Marta.

This morning I begin the journey that I should have taken
so long ago. I will find an intense and vibrant world. I will
make my place in it. I know you will follow in my footsteps
one day, and shape a meaningful life for yourself.

Love,
Mama

Underneath:

Forgive me. May God give us strength.

And below that, in thick, smeared ink, her full married
name.

Merisa Lara Ostentuin

She remembered to leave that behind.

The postcard lay under the letter. It had come right on time, ten
years to the day. What kind of twisted miracle was that?
Inexplicable chance had dropped my mother's cheap message
through a narrow one-day time slot, landing a claim to perfect

pathos and pain. How could I not read it? My mother had played this card to perfection.

She had remarried, she wrote. She had children, new children. How was I keeping, and how was my father?

No return address. A postmark, *"Los Angeles,"* in blue.

I sat on my bed and fingered the postcard, skating over its scenery. I smelled the words it presented, the chosen words. They didn't smell of freedom.

I lay down with the card pressed between my palms, between my knees. I was feeling something, to be certain. I was sure of it, of something.

I imagined her in her new life, living among bolts of silk and wool that smelled of chemical dyes, their fibres on the air, vaguely on the tongue, catching in the throat. Sewing for wealthy American ladies. Exhausting her dreams to rear new children. Her children.

Perhaps those children, too, would hold the damning message in their eyes. *I could see that I should.*

I smiled, the muscles of my lips feeling cruel. I waited for anger and vengeance to wash through me.

I held the card until I ran out of patience. There were no answers there.

The apartment was terribly quiet. I pictured my father sitting, still and silent, at the table.

I had thought him powerless and wounded, blind to his own failings, too bland for his worldly wife. I had thought it was he who had driven my mother out of our home. I'd pitied him and I had protected him from my pity.

Now I knew that he had been deceiving me. Siding with my mother. Collaborating with her.

Pitying me.

He had known all along: I had shaped my mother's departure, had blessed it with my eyes.

He waited for my response, his ten-year task complete.

I was trapped in my room with my postcard, with my letter, with my shifting life.

∞

The past rewrote itself in my sleep as I drifted into dusk clutching the card. I unearthed the script of my childhood and laid it into my mother's tight loops of ballpoint ink. I read it again; I read it for the first time. I saw it whole: my young life cracked open in a new language and revealed as a work of naïveté. The translation came easily.

I saw now that I had been waiting all those years, expecting something. Now I had received it and could expect nothing more.

This was my mother's gift to me: her courage, her flight, her freedom. She had done it for me, because of me. And in return, there were things she asked of me: to prove her noble, to dream, to escape. To risk being alone.

But I would not be alone, especially not for her.

An image came back to me of the mother I thought I'd known: a woman strong and passionate, fierce in her talent. Though her words were often sharp, it had been her silences that punished. There had been no peace in her quiet.

She ran her sewing machine like a team of rowing slaves, pushing the fabric, pushing her foot on the pedal, rushing off the edge in a tangle of threads that she sliced at once with her sharp shears. Leaping up without sliding back her chair when there was a seam to be ironed open or closed. She sewed as though she herself were running, running to the wall she faced with her head down.

But when she taught me to sew, she taught a craft of patience and care: "Let the machine take the fabric, Marta. That's it. Slow. Press now with your foot, just a little. Slide your fingers out of the way . . . Now press."

I remembered her as exacting, yet she seldom voiced expectations. They were in her eyes. They were between her words.

"Let's make me a dress from this, Mama."

"Don't be ridiculous. That's lining."

I had thought that I was living a life she would be proud to return to and join. That I had made life my own, had enjoyed freedom within its borders. Now I burned with embarrassment. I had lived a pretense. With teenage clarity, I saw that there was no freedom: there was only a stitching together of pain and blame.

I wore this truth like a shabby coat, wore with tragedy and pride its wrinkles and dragging sleeves. In it, I became the person I was meant to be: abandoned, deceived, tired.

My girlfriends, barely out of their teens, had already all settled on husbands. Their jobs were not much different from mine, but I saw now that their attitudes were much more realistic. They knew the world for what it was: a place where a girl seeks approval before cutting her hair, where dishes and bedsheets must be endlessly washed and washed, where news never surprises or informs.

I sank into real life.

∽

In the heat of the bakery, every task became pointless, hope-less. Cravings echoed through me. I had no name for them. I yearned to gorge myself on my failings, to pack them like gauze in all my hollow spaces—around my eyes, between my lungs, in the ventricles of my heart. I yearned to fail.

"Fräulein," Zach called when he heard me enter in the mornings, "where's my sunshine? Come into the back. You make the panini today. Forget your troubles. Why should you have troubles! You need more sleep. You need more happiness. Such a young girl like you."

I quit but didn't go far. There was a café next door. I made it my vocation to sit there, watching the street. There was nothing to wait for—that was key in my new cache of truths. And yet I sat waiting.

∽

Then a husband was delivered to me. Clutch, grab, thrust. He was far away, in the States like my mother, yet he was already as good as mine.

He came to me via another item on my pillow. This one I snatched up without hesitation. It was a plane ticket. Five days in Los Angeles: another surprise from my father. Another gift.

My father thought I should find my mother. I went to find my own sort of answer.

I found Kurt.

8

THE BRAND NEW AMERICAN GIRLFRIENDS I met in the hotel in Los Angeles heard my story and were impressed.

We sat drinking in a small bar. The girls looked away as they talked, all three of them exchanging sensual glances with a sharp-looking, dark-haired man who stood carefully relaxed against the opposite wall, his leather jacket opening over a crisp grey T-shirt.

Carrie shook her head. "God, imagine. I've got a nine-year-old niece. If my sister-in-law left like that, I'd kill her."

The two others were both named Chelsea. "Yeah, sure, if you wanted to find her first," said one. "But Marta's not gonna lower herself to look."

"You think you can find anyone in L.A. anyway? It's all unlisted numbers and—"

"She said she's not looking. She's not gonna beg."

My finger chased drops of dew down my beer glass. I *could* look for my mother. Maybe she—

"I mean, she didn't even give her address, right? That's such a slap in the face. It's so low, don't you think?"

"Totally. A total slap. Like, 'Oh, hi, I guess I have to write but screw you anyway.'"

"It wasn't like that," I said.

"'I got my lovely L.A. life here. Who needs you?'"

"Omigod, I know. My mom totally started hating me when I hit my teens. Just ask her. Soon as I—"

"Think she's a movie star?"

"My *mom*?"

"No, twit. Marta's mother."

My glass was still empty. I craned my head, searching for our latest order. "She's a seamstress," I said.

The table fell silent.

Then a Chelsea piped up. "Here's our beer. The Bud's mine. She gets that one. Yeah. Okay: To freedom."

"Bottoms up."

I lifted my drink as the man smiled in our direction. His satisfied grin slid over us. It lingered on me.

My hair was long then. Its heavy curls closed in around my face no matter how often I pushed them off my forehead. My baby fat had become curving buttocks and breasts whose fullness astounded me. An even bigger surprise: I had cheekbones, collarbones, hipbones.

I had cleavage. As I tipped my beer glass, the right side of my bra raised a breast for Kurt's eyes. Within the splaying angle of my bronze V-neck, the hollow between my breasts became a dark, deep cleft.

I glanced across to see Kurt staring, his lips loose. I turned away, but had to look back. I liked watching Kurt wanting me.

I tried to look blasé, but he mimicked my pout. I pulled my lips into primness and sat straighter. When I glanced at him again, his eyes were serious, intense. I raised an eyebrow. He raised an eyebrow.

I was hooked.

The girlfriends leaned over our table of beer glasses, gasping above the foamy heads.

"Gorgeous, don't you think? Really hot, right?"

"Truly, Mart, he's your type. You need someone like that, get your bootstraps up."

"Your garters."

"Omigod! He'd be amazing, don't you think? He'd love that stuff, don't you think?"

"For sure he likes leather."

"He's got a motorcycle. Right? You think? Is that helmet hair or what?"

"Bed head. That sleepy-edgy look."

"Marta? What do you think? He's older, but—"

"She doesn't care about that. The older the better. The best lay I—"

"You have to talk to him. One night, Marta, that's all you need. Believe me. I've been there."

Their voices chorused: "One night."

Three hands went up around me, each crooking a finger to Kurt.

His stride was a work of cockiness. He was thirty, I would learn, but he walked like a smooth-hipped boy.

"Ladies," he murmured, rounding the table. "A pleasure." He slid across the bench seat to bump his hip against mine.

I raised my glass and sipped the velvet off.

Kurt's hair tumbled into choppy layers that covered the tops of his ears. His skin was pale, with a flush of fresh sun across the bridge of his nose and his cheekbones. His eyes seemed to be blue, though I was too close to glance casually to check.

He sat shoulder to shoulder with me, one finger tapping compulsively on an unlit cigarette. Laughing, he leaned into me, and his keenly seductive scent pulled me closer.

The girls did the speaking, telling Kurt that "Marta loves tall men. She's only . . . I dunno how tall. Anyhow, it's all the same when you're horizontal." And "She doesn't talk much, but it isn't the talking that's important. If she doesn't show you herself, I wouldn't mind."

These brazen, barefaced girls. Did they think they were daring, sowing their oats in California? This was for them just another American holiday in their carefree American lives. They all swam in the same water, breathed the same air. They knew nothing of my dark Canadian winters, of grey afternoons among silver-grey limestone buildings, of sitting in the shade of maples while passing rowers carve freshwater trails in the still-ness. They knew nothing of me—only my story of maternal abandonment, of the search I had no intention of undertaking.

The girls had chosen Kurt for me. I was the lucky winner in their audacious, smutty game, but I was not one of them. Unlike them, I was living a true adventure tonight. I was expe-riencing another life on that strange evening, and I could make it whatever I wished.

Kurt, taking a vacation between jobs, was Canadian like me. Kurt wanted me.

I laughed aloud. Why shouldn't I have this Kurt? This was what I'd come for, I knew it: to take what I wanted. To reshape my life, my way.

I turned to speak to him.

Immediately he ducked his head and spoke in my ear. "Come on, Marta. You're better than all this silly gab. Let's get out of here, get some air."

His fingers moved heavily across my thighs, searching for my hands which I held clasped in my lap. I let him pry them apart and entwine his large fingers with my own. I closed my mouth. My lips, suddenly, were swollen with wanting.

The air outside was thick with humidity. The metal door closed on the sounds of the bar, leaving me standing against Kurt in the pounding quiet.

Everything seemed unfamiliar in the most enticing way. The air itself was different, with unfamiliar possibilities suspended in its moist molecules. A space had opened up between worlds, and I was itching to own it.

We left Kurt's rental car parked on the street, the better to caress and mouth each other as we stumbled toward his hotel.

Kurt hesitated at his hotel room door.

I thought he was hoping to seduce me in the hallway. "Inside," I said, and he obeyed.

We stripped in a hurry, trapping fabric between our impatient bodies. We fell onto the bed and teased the remains of clothing off sensitized limbs. My skin flushed under Kurt's rough hands. He spread his hot breath across my thighs.

Then he slipped into the bathroom, leaving me shaking on mangled bedding, stunned with desire.

The shower started up.

"Kurt?"

He did not emerge.

"Kurt?"

I sprang to my feet, flinging covers to the floor, and stomped into the bathroom.

He was at the sink.

"What are you doing?" I demanded.

"Don't let the steam out."

"Fuck the steam." I knew this game: draw me close and drop me.

"Needed a Tylenol," Kurt said.

"And a shower?" I yanked the curtain and glared.

Kurt's eyes didn't meet mine. His gaze roamed over me, and I followed it.

Even I could see that the pink glow across my chest had intensified. That the anger in my lungs lifted my breasts in a rhythm beyond my control. That I was naked and nineteen and my skin gleamed.

I bent to shut off the water. As I stood again, I stretched languorously, lifting my arms and rolling my shoulders, releasing the tension in my spine.

Kurt's eyes followed my body.

I crossed my arms below my breasts and barely parted my legs.

His Adam's apple leapt.

My eyes went to the towel tucked around his hips.

Kurt reached behind him and gripped the sink. He leaned back. Where the strands of his curls touched the foggy mirror, drops stroked silver on the whitened glass.

I felt my bare soles lifting toward him.

I worked the towel apart. My fingers slipped down his damp abdomen, and he rose to meet them.

I returned alone to Kingston, returned home to my father, burdened with his expectations. I had nothing to say to him.

Why would I have sought my mother? What good would it have done?

Why did he stand before me and wear his wishes in his eyes?

He had chosen for me a decade of innocence and ignorance, then assumed I would bring home answers. I'd found what I'd gone for. It was neither innocence nor a reprise of my mother's rejection.

My assignment was complete. I had all I needed in the way of answers. Why, now, should I enlighten my father? I didn't so much as hint.

9

I BUY A ROLL of clear packing tape and use it to repair the spines of Mrs. Oland's books, books neither of us have any intention of reading. Romance paperbacks, Christian books, *How to Beat the Arthritis Odds,* squat encyclopedias in gold and red, an extensive collection from the Canadian Centennial Library. I riffle through *The Canadian Look,* published the year after my birth. There's "The Polar Look," "The Sporting Look," "The Look That Could Only Happen Here." No white polyester slacks with cut-outs at the ankles. No negative circles in "Shapes to Tell a Nation By."

For sealing up boxes we use beige masking tape. I pick at the end and yank lengths from the coil. I wear the roll on my wrist. Like elongated puzzle pieces, extra strips dangle from my arm. I choose one as required. It pulls the skin, tugs out fine hairs. I yearn for physical sensation, for tension and release.

℘

Mrs. Oland's bathroom is pink—the tiles, the towels, and two china figurines: a girl in a pinafore flashing ruffled panties as one ankle-socked foot kicks up, and a pink dog that resembles a skinny horse.

I don't like figurines, but I appreciate the shiny black sole of the pinafore girl's shoe. I picture kerchiefed European ladies painting her and grumbling; other figures' shoe bottoms don't need paint.

I feel like a kerchief lady myself these days. My hair is lustreless, unevenly shoulder length and fighting against the bobby pins I've borrowed from Mrs. Oland's bathroom. My curves spreading under loose clothing could be those of a woman twice my age. My hands are dry on my skin, on the pads of my hips and soft thighs.

In the shower I comb my fingers through my pubic hair. I reach low, dipping and rubbing, until my moisture commingles with the shower spray and the frustration becomes too much.

I lean my head against the wet tile wall. I berate myself for my need.

10

PANTING PHONE CALLS, Halifax-to-Kingston. Letters.

Dear Marta,

It's official. I got the Toronto job. It's a big leap—major salary, real responsibility. I'm management. No shit! I'm coming to Toronto—and Kingston—on August 3rd. I'll phone before then. Looking forward to seeing you. Got to see you. I'll come from the airport, right from the plane. Meet me at the train station—I'll phone, we'll work out the details. What you should wear and not wear. No flat shoes!!!

xox
Kurt

No one had wanted me that way before. No one had given me that power.

⁊

The day of Kurt's arrival, I shopped for shoes and lingerie in a gale of excitement, then dumped the bags in my room, scared.

My father arrived as I entered the kitchen to get a drink. I told him a friend was coming to see me that evening, that I wouldn't be home until late.

He sat down and crossed his legs. "Kurt Fett? Who is Kurt Fett?"

"I met him in California."

My father looked at his golden leather slippers which were upside down in the hallway. He looked toward the door with its three locks.

"A boyfriend," he said softly. "This Kurt is your boyfriend."

"So?"

"You say nothing about your mother but you go get a boyfriend."

"What I do about my mother is my business."

"It's family business."

"Abandonment isn't 'family.'"

"Marta, it was the seventies."

"So?"

"Everyone left in the seventies. Wives—"

"That's how you see it?"

"I was good to your mother. She wanted to go. She wanted to divorce. Should I blame myself?"

"You can't blame anyone. Not her, not me."

He shook his head. "I don't blame you."

"You kept the letter."

"That was the plan. In ten years you would be nineteen, and I would—"

"I know the plan. The plan was bad. The plan stank. Don't you get it? The plan hurt."

"Oh, *hurt*. Come on, Marta. Let the pain go. It's like rain: It can feed the plants or destroy the plants. You need to bend and—"

"Don't tell me what I need. I'm not the one in denial."

"What's there to deny?"

"How about your whole life?"

He picked invisible lint off his sock. "The past is past."

"You feel nothing," I snapped. "'Let the pain go.' Everything rolls off your back." I grabbed a can of cream soda from the fridge and threw the door closed. "Me included."

∞

While my father and I fought, Kurt landed at the Toronto airport.

He came to me clean-shaven despite the flight and the train trip to Kingston. He'd smoothed the scratchy jaw that had burned my thighs and raked my nipples. He came smelling of citrus and oriental spice: the smell of a hotel room, the smell of a man travelling on business.

I met him at the train station, and we hurried to my father's walk-up apartment. I was insistent.

Kurt sang in a low voice as I led him to the door. He pressed against me as I slipped the key into the lock and turned the handle. A fit of giggles spluttered behind my hand. The door opened and we stumbled into the living room.

We stood and kissed, hard and long, then I pulled him into my bedroom.

When I let go, his hands flew to his silver belt buckle, to the straining zipper of his jeans. I closed the door and stood with my back against it, feeling a rush rise from the curving arches of my feet up through my entire body.

My father would hear us tonight.

I knew he would do nothing. He had not stopped my mother. He had not stopped her for me.

I would not stop for him.

I lost something that night. I tumbled away from something as Kurt and I grappled in my own small bed, below the magazine images of Günter Grass and Expressionist art taped level on my walls. As Kurt entered me and left his liquid there, I too, for fleeting minutes, abandoned something to him.

I felt its absence despite the rampage of blood into muscle, the surge of hormones, the creaking of the mattress and frame. Released by the heat of Kurt's skin on my skin, I felt blessedly, briefly, free.

In those remarkable minutes, I felt separated from my history.

I could have thought this: *What's the point of holding on to a past, and the rewrite of that past, and the acid repercussions of that past, if one can lose one's consciousness so completely with a lover? Why bother lugging chains that are so easily shrugged off? If sex—so ludicrously rough and earnest—can make one forget oneself, then where is the nobility in believing oneself scarred?*

I could have thought this: *Why desire meaning? Why carry the memory of pain?*

I could have.

I thought this: *Sex is everything. Concise, complete, effective.*

My father did not enter or knock. He didn't come to the bedroom door. He would not risk seeing me naked or dishevelled or unprepared. In his universe, things were orderly and reasonable; softness wore down mountains and fashioned keys to softer worlds. It seemed, at first, that I had not changed this.

He waited until after my lover left in the early morning, until after I'd slept again clutching the sweat-clammy pillow, until it was past time for me to rise and make breakfast.

He waited until it became clear that I would not be appearing in the kitchen.

Then the apartment suddenly roared.

Music blasted from the dining room, dramatic orchestral sound. I bolted from my room, my heart pounding.

My father sat at the kitchen table, his back straight, his face impassive, his gaze locked directly ahead. He had not fetched the morning paper. The table in front of him was bare save for his trembling hands.

He sat with the radio behind him, a forceful fall of sound rushing about him.

I reached for the radio, and silence flooded back.

For a moment my father did nothing. Then he closed his eyes. He bent his head. Raising his hands, he covered his ears.

Thus he sat, with me standing staring at him, until I left the room.

He sat while I dressed.

He sat while I left the apartment.

I spent the day window shopping, nibbling on fast food, and calling girlfriends from pay phones.

Hearing of my daring night with Kurt, they squealed with excitement. "You've got guts, Marta! Way to stand up to your father. Way to show him you're not under his thumb any more."

But they didn't know: I had never been under my father's thumb. I had only been protecting him. When I had cooked his meals, when I had laundered his clothing, when I had answered his silence with gentle silence, I had only been sheltering him. Not only from my mother, but also from myself, from the pity I felt for him.

These friends knew nothing of the letters that revealed his deception. They didn't know how he'd kept my mother's words from me, how he'd played it her way, made himself accept her ways and expected me to do the same.

No one could understand what it meant to have slept with Kurt under my father's roof. They saw only a nineteen-year-old's reckless joyride toward freedom—just a crazy story to whisper one day, cackling with delight and shock, in our old age.

∾

Kurt took the job and proposed marriage. I could think of no reason to refuse.

We played house in a Toronto motel for a few weeks. Kurt was at half-salary, meeting his colleagues, attending preliminary training and assessment sessions. He bought a used car, an old burgundy sedan.

"We'll trade it in when I get my first bonus. Ha! We'll throw it out and buy an import."

I made tissue paper carnations for its hood.

I planned the wedding in fruitless long-distance discussions with my Kingston girlfriends. They crooned for a crown of flowers, a veil dotted with pearls, a chorus line of brides-maids in lime-green sequined satin. "What could be sexier?" They pictured a wedding to lust for.

I was hoping to move beyond lust.

If not for my impending marriage, my mother's sewing machine would have stayed behind in my father's home. Instead, I had dragged the dusty case from the back corner of a closet and brought it to Toronto.

Surely I could open it without resurrecting the old ache for my mother. I could sew without honouring her memory; I wouldn't even think of her. I had a wedding dress to make. A wedding would change everything.

In our motel room I cut fabric and paper patterns on the bed while the iron whined on the dresser. On a table too low for my knees, I set up the machine. I pressed the foot pedal, and the room filled with the humming voice of childhood.

My stitches looped crazily at first. When I bent lower to peer at them, my hair cascaded onto the machine. The sewing machine could consume me, could drink me in by the hair.

I jerked up straight. In the tackle box which rattled with sewing tools and accessories, I dug out Jack the Ripper. The tool was smaller than I remembered. I snapped apart my lunatic stitches and eased out the fragments of thread. Then I stopped and took a long, deep breath. I spent a minute just stroking the fabric, my wedding fabric.

I adjusted the thread tension. I was in control. With my back hunched and sore, I sewed a simple wedding suit—a pale blue bolero jacket, collarless blouse, and mid-calf skirt—and planned my future.

I wanted a city hall service with a witness—any witness— and a binding contract. I wanted that paper in my fist. Wanted proof that I'd finally—good riddance—closed the door on the growing-up stage of my life.

I found myself running to greet Kurt when he got home, taking his hands in mine, words tumbling out before I could stop them.

"I'm going to buy the flowers at the corner, I've decided. It'll all be over before you know it. You don't have to do a thing. I've got it all figured out. Don't worry, you won't have to get a tux—but maybe a yellow flower in your lapel, a yellow rose, a little yellow—"

Kurt was amenable. He was charming.

"Marta," he said daily, "how did I live without you?"

I would search for the irony in his eyes.

❦

Now Mrs. Oland asks the same question and my eyes well in anger, for what kind of aid do I give her? Encouraging her in her charade of influence. Pretending she will ever make a difference to anyone. Acting as though what I feel for her is love.

I know love. I have known love. No one can tell me this is it. A cup of tea, black, with sugar. A new pile of newspapers brought inside. A gentle pat of my hand on her liver-spotted forearm.

Love? I could just as soon slap her, and I suspect I one day will.

11

THAT SEPTEMBER I turned twenty and was married at city hall.

I, Marta, took Kurt to be my husband, my dearly beloved, till death do us part, rest in peace.

I married Kurt with a sour-faced girlfriend at my side. She had brought her young son, hoping to slip him in as a ring bearer, but I was too preoccupied to get the rings into his hand. The officiator and his assistant watched me and Kurt kiss. Their smiles were bored. My impatience had rubbed off on them.

Within days we were driving through battered farmlands seeking Restive, a town northwest of Toronto. It was all there: a small row house that abutted the sidewalk, a string of neighbouring homes insulating the walls, a telecommunications software firm with a desk for Kurt.

Restive had an ornamental old Main Street and a new shopping mall. It was ringed with farms and industrial construction. I could borrow a bike and ride past fields of sheep, hop a bus to the Sears store, window shop for old-fashioned teddy bears, or sit on a bench in one of three well-cared-for parks where I could meet other young women like me—transplants waiting to root. I could buy fabric, and sew curtains, slipcovers, and tablecloths in Miami pastel hues. I could transform everything within our walls.

I did none of these things.

That fall I stood for hours at the back window, eager for nothing yet awash with yearning. Restless but riveted in the kitchen, clutching a cup of acidic black coffee, I pondered the language of our new home. Kurt's playful teasing was interspersed with cruelty: a sneering tone, the gripping of my wrist, scornful indifference.

I thought about the precision of his words. They were sharp and intentional. Only when he forgot himself did they pour forth in ugliness. Only when he drank did he raise his voice.

He had a bar toy, a plastic bird that bobbed rhythmically, its beak dipping into a glass of water. It would hesitate as it feigned drinking, then rush upwards, back to the height of its arc and beyond, where it gazed at our stucco ceiling—only to let its head fall forward, once more, and more, and again.

I sat tapping its red shorn-velvet head. I moved it from room to room, keeping it in motion between passes of the vacuum cleaner, between the rinse of a plate and the soaping of a mug, between thrusts of a paper towel across a mirror.

There was something in its perpetual dance, a promise of something. Or there was something in its slowing that made me panic, made me reach out and tap its head. *Drink, bird. Drink.*

∞

When Kurt left the car at home for the day, I shopped at the grocery store in the mall, slipping around the aisles as though on ice skates. When I returned and emptied the crinkling plastic bags into the fridge and cupboards, stashing the onions under the kitchen sink, I could barely wait to discover what I'd brought home. Sliced sandwich meats, sliced cheeses, huge soft buns that opened like mouths under my fingers. I would spread thick butter and brown mustard, spear pickles, and open jars of fat olives. I would eat with eyes closed in pleasure, wash my single plate by hand, and feel as though I'd stolen a full, deep belly of life.

Then, inevitably, my gut would cramp. My lungs would stiffen.

I needed something. Something more. What I had was all in a pantry or a fridge.

∞

Kurt started off slowly at the new company, cycling through a few days in various departments to experience the flavour of the firm before officially assuming his managerial position.

There were benign moments at home. Kurt watched television and laughed at the weekend comic strips. He was sometimes enticing: raising a delighted eyebrow at the curve of my breasts in a sweater, slipping his arms around me from behind, then walking his fingers up my arms while I tried to push him away before the tickling began.

He assembled his free weights in the living room and explained his lifting techniques, speaking in a monotone as he slowly raised a barbell. When my attention wandered, he tossed a five-pound iron weight toward my feet.

He started a jigsaw puzzle, sitting with a cigarette between his fingers and a beer at his feet, his face relaxed above the jumble of colours spread on our glass-topped coffee table. I walked around him, careful not to disturb him as he daydreamed over the emerging image.

At the end of the afternoon, he swept the unfinished puzzle into its box. He snapped on the TV as though he had no choice, as though he realized he had to come home.

At work, he shrugged away the incomprehensibility of the processes he was meant to be learning. He laughed about it all.

"Charm, Marta. That's the ticket. A smile, a firm hand-shake, and my irresistible boyish charm."

"That'll take you far as a manager. Was that what you used to launch your software thing in Halifax?"

"Yeah. Boyish charm and ridiculous amounts of start-up capital. Beautiful on paper. Know what it was, that company? Four guys in a garage, running extension cords from the house."

"That was good enough for someone to buy you out."

"Back then you could slap the words 'user-friendly' on a paper clip and someone would buy you out."

"It was good enough to get you this job."

"Yeah." He laughed. "That's the rich part."

But by the end of Kurt's two weeks of rotating assign-ments, the laughter stopped.

"They cut my salary. I haven't even started and they cut my salary."

"How can they do that?"

"They're reorganizing. They say I'm on probation, that I'm not really hired yet. They're not even letting me get down to the job, and they cut my frigging salary!"

I took his hand. "We don't need all that money, anyway."

"It's not the money!"

"I'm sure it's not about you. You know these high-tech places. They're so up and down. There are always layoffs and—"

"There's no frigging way they're laying me off. I come all the way from Halifax, I get goddamn married, and—"

"What does marriage have to do with it?"

"I'm a manager. I'm supposed to be a goddamned manager."

I took my hand away, crossed my arms.

"Don't look at me like that. You and those bastards. Bitches. That one in my department. *My* department. Treating me like some loser."

"You're not a loser."

"Oh, thank you very frigging much. As if you'd know."

He began his real job, his permanent managerial position. I had expected him to walk in and draw all the developers to himself through the force of his gravitational pull. Instead, they continued to orbit in their independent galaxies. Kurt showed me how they swatted him away, heads down, fingers flying.

He was too proud to raise the matter outright with higher management, but he slipped veiled questions toward his boss, a woman hardly older than me. ("She's a pup," he had told me, "a bitch pup.")

He relayed her words to me that evening, mimicking in a high, hard voice, his hands on his hips, his face twisting. "'I do understand, Kurt, that it isn't easy for an entrepreneur to join an established corporation. Fortunately we're very training-oriented. I recommend our workshops Mastering Fears and Frustrations, and I'm Okay When You're Okay.'" He snivelled in falsetto, "'They'll help you re-engineer your bonding paradigm.'"

I laughed.

Kurt's hand swung out fast and hard and struck me in the mouth.

(*"How old, how sweet."*)

❧

He barely spoke of his job after that. He didn't need to. I saw what he was becoming.

He would slip out for cigarettes and come home hours later, drunk. He would call to say he was working late and come home before dawn, staggering, stinking. He stopped calling altogether, stopped making excuses for his drunkenness.

He was already a decade older than me, and his handsome face aged ten years beyond that.

❧

The dark days of November rolled through me in churning waves of nausea. And no wonder: I was pregnant. I held off telling Kurt for as long as possible, waiting for—I don't know what. Epiphany? Change?

Even I knew there was no point in hoping for change.

It hardly mattered. Already the roiling in my gut had dulled my sensitivity to Kurt's nastiness. I had all but stopped caring what he thought of me. I felt fat, my hair hung in ropy strands, but I cared about nothing beyond my nausea and the baby that was the cause of it.

I took time to choose my moment and release my news. By January my queasiness cleared. I emerged from it as though I were the one being born: newly aware. Eager to welcome myself back to full life.

One snowy night Kurt came home barely bleary. His jaw was slack; his eyes seemed focused inward, bewildered.

I spoke without empathy, without the anticipation of regret or the fear of retaliation. My body surged with heat. Only my voice was cold.

"I'm pregnant, Kurt. I'm going to be a mother." (Aim, thrust, *twist*.) "You'll have a baby to support soon. So chin up. It's back to work tomorrow."

I stood tall before him.

He raised his hands slowly and dragged his palms over his face. His heavy eyes roamed my body. His mouth formed a resigned smile. He turned to leave the room, but I took hold of his arm. I pressed against him.

We made love.

I called it *love*. I pulled him into me. I made him last; I arched in pleasure and triumph. I knew it could be the last time for a long time. Not because of safety, not to spare the child bursting to life inside me, but because Kurt would not want me now, now that he had seen what I was capable of.

I had stood up to him. I had told him; I had done it perfectly. I had told him with the power of conception in my womb.

I was charged with life, given a future. I could think again and see clearly.

As Kurt slept and I lay beside him, my fingers tracing shapes on my belly, I resolved not to worry about what was to come. I would live here with my child. Kurt would come and go. He would not touch me in anger now; he was cruel, but he was cautious in his own way, and he was not entirely indecent.

I would stop worrying about the security of his job. He could still turn on the charm. He must have been participating in meetings, he must have been generating ideas and making contributions. He still had the guts to follow his own rules, and he was still always certain he was right.

I wouldn't leave him, wouldn't disappear. I wouldn't have to now. I would have a purpose outside us, beyond him.

I lay thinking of the child. Andrew? Carina? Sophie? Alexander? Alana?

Asha?

12

Occasionally, in those early months, I drove to Kingston and back, all between nine and five of a working day. I brought my father food, things I had cooked or baked, things that kept well.

I delivered them unannounced, arriving when I suspected he'd be out with his coveralls and brushes. I discarded his aging leftovers, casseroles hardly touched, and took the empty serving dishes. I left before he came home. On the few occasions when our paths intersected—barely touching cheeks in the hallway, or nodding awkwardly at one another as I knelt at the open fridge—he never spoke of his life and I never spoke of mine. I did not suggest he eat more of my food, and he did not ask that I return his key.

"How is it going?" he had asked one day in November, catching me outside the apartment.

"Fine. You?" I tugged my coat closed.

He nodded. "The same."

"Fine, too? Or same as always?"

"Fine. As always."

A twinge of old anger flared. "You're always fine. So you say."

He rocked on his heels. "Should I complain?"

A cold wind swirled dry leaves onto our shoes. I held my collar against my throat and thought about my father marking papers through the winter. Had he forgotten how torturous it would be?

"How are you getting by?" I asked.

"The painting has been good. Getting cold now." He switched his coveralls from one arm to the other and back again. "Your mother sent some money."

"She sent you money?" A tug in my belly.

(*"Don't yank the thread, Marta, you'll break it! If you can't pull it gently—"*)

He nodded. "I guess you want to read the note."

"What does it say?"

"She feels guilty."

"Right."

"She isn't a bad person. She's stubborn, but—"

"Don't."

"She loved you. *Loves* you."

I looked away.

"I wouldn't lie to you, Marta."

"Wouldn't you? For her?"

"You're more like her than you think."

"Just stop. Okay? I need to get back."

"She's wealthy. Her husband—"

"No return address?"

"No return address."

"I left something in the fridge. Forty-five minutes, three hundred degrees."

"There's also money for you, Marta."

"No."

"Quite a lot. You might need it one day."

"You use it." I felt in my purse for the car key.

"Put it into an account; just leave it there."

"Don't want it."

"You never know what will happen with Kurt."

"I don't care."

"I'll mail you the cheque." He pushed open the door. A gust of leaves scuttled after him.

13

THE GARDEN IS MRS. OLAND'S TERRITORY. She likes to sit by the willow tree in the backyard, her eyes half shut, her fingers rubbing the hollow beside her bony left thumb. I don't disturb her in her reveries. I don't even enter the yard after I've made sure she's safely settled in the folding wooden lawn chair with its striped cushion of faded tangerine and pink. This is the only place where I see her truly relaxed and unveiled to the world. I suspect this is her real church.

A few of the parishioners from St. Boniface used to come and mow the grass, pushing ahead despite Mrs. Oland's protests. But they found themselves the object of verbal sniping that escalated on occasion to disconcertingly bold insults, even the odd flaring of fury.

"I told Annie Greszlo to pack it up and get the Hades off of my property," Mrs. Oland told me. "Raised my voice to her, very sharp. They had a little meeting about me then. They all thought I was unsound, becoming an infant in my old age. No one likes when an old person takes control."

She fixed me with an intense look and leaned her head toward mine. "You pay a price for people's kindness, Marta. Let them help, and they expect you to need them."

She still rejects would-be gardeners in terse phone conversations and standoffs.

An attempt is made by an older man whom I've never seen at church. He knocks unexpectedly at the side door.

"Please tell Mrs. Oland that Lawrence Edgar is here," he says, eyeing me suspiciously. "I'll get the lawn and back garden cleaned up and slip away. No need for her to come out. I know where to find everything."

When I relay the message, Mrs. Oland's spoon clatters into her fruit salad cup. She stretches out her hand, beckoning for my arm.

"My daughter's husband. Ex-husband. A meddler. Always was." She unhooks her cane from the back of the chair and steers me to the door. "'Slip out.' As if I asked him to come in the first place! You get him over here, Marta, and we'll set him straight."

I fetch him. His distrust of me is plain on his face, but it fades as he nears Mrs. Oland.

"Lawrence," she tells him, "I am not well. I simply can't have you clanging about my property whenever it suits you."

Perhaps he is prepared for this. He flares his nostrils and takes a deep breath.

"We're worried about you," he begins. "Mrs. Hunter told Yolanda that you hung up on her. You won't let Helen and Frank bring you your groceries any more. And apparently you haven't called any of your friends to take you to your doctor's appointments; people are worried you've stopped going."

"My doctor's appointments are my business."

"We only want to help you. Sometimes you need to let people help. We would feel better."

"Ah. You would feel better."

"We are your family."

"You are not my family any more, Lawrence. You seem to forget that."

"Well, I still worry about you. You should listen to Yolanda. She, at least, appreciates that I'm trying to keep an eye on—"

"You'll want to be going now." It looks as if the head will snap off the cane in her tight grip.

He hesitates. "Perhaps it's a question of influence. Until now, you've always been so careful of whom you associated with."

"Perhaps not careful enough."

Lawrence stands silent for a moment. He says, "Well, then. If you need anything."

"I have Marta."

Accusation stretches between his rigid back and my stock-still body.

∽

I have gardening to do. Cooking, cleaning, packing, labelling, gardening. To qualify: subsistence cooking, light cleaning, endless packing, repetitive labelling, and discreet, sensitive gardening.

I have paper. My twin-sized maplewood bed, here in the basement, has a small dresser to match. In the top drawer I found airmail tissue. Now I lie on my side with the tablet open to a clean sheet. I hold a pen.

I would make a mark, but who is there to receive it?

There is no address book in my bedroom, no friendly notes in my bag. In my wallet is a health insurance card, a credit

card, a small ad from a local clothing store. I have four parishioners' phone numbers and Mrs. Oland's doctor's card. A
library card. A business card of Kurt's. I have a driver's licence
but no car, the car I once drove to Loblaws, to department
stores, to a bus station to buy tickets. I have one unused ticket
to Toronto and a stub.

If I were Mrs. Oland, I would know what to do with these
things.

Mrs. Oland is napping and the house sits in calcifying
calm. I walk out to the shed for a weeding tool and head to the
front lawn.

I am bending over dandelions when an unearthly roar hits
my ears. I spin toward the source.

What I see freezes time. Huge and low above the roof floats
a hot-air balloon. It hangs motionless, suspended by nothing.

For a moment I think I have called for it.

For a moment there is no sky.

The balloon fills everything with its silent form. Its red
and yellow stripes tower wide and high. In its basket three
passengers stand. They seem as close to me as I am to myself,
close enough to reach.

The flame blasts again. The enormous balloon rises. It
drifts mutely out of view, drifts and disappears.

Then the roar resounds a third and fainter final time.

I stare at the empty air, mesmerized.

A balloon. Three people.

One of them lifted a hand to me, silent against the fire
against the sky.

∽

Things I left behind in Restive: two bedrooms, two beds, one bathroom, one kitchen, one mudroom, one basement, four closets.

Ground-in dirt on the knees of Asha's pants. Kurt's socks, inside out, kicked in among the shoes. Sweater shoulders stretching into shapes of wire hangers, apple core in Kleenex in raincoat pocket (mine), saltscapes white on leather boots, piled-up hats too warm, too tight, too sweat-stained.

Scent of Kurt.

Photos: Kurt previously handsome, dark-haired, curling lashes, pale blue eyes, flat cheekbones, grinding teeth in muscle-clenched jaw.

Cigarette butts. Beer bottles, liquor bottles, scent of vomit on my husband's lips.

Sweet lips of Asha. Her knees. Her shoulder blades. Her fine brown hair.

Snippet of baby hair in tinfoil in envelope under mattress on bed.

An inventory of bankruptcy.

∞

I drop the weeding tool and do not bend to pick it up. If I reach for it now, the vessel of my heart will tip and spill.

∞

Dear Asha—

14

It was as I had predicted: Kurt quieted while my body grew the life within it. I gave up the leanness I'd honed in my teenage years. My breasts and belly spread, rising as generously as yeast dough, until my abdomen hardened and pushed forward in aggressive growth.

I worked hard preparing a nursery fit for my developing child. When I'd exhausted all the decorating ideas in the public library, I bought acrylic paints and experimented on paper, mixing penny-sized daubs of colour and letting my imagination spread them on walls.

The child's room would be yellow, but which yellow? I rejected lemon for its snideness and primary yellow for its stubborn glee. I craved something light and buttery, but by the time I finished tweaking and softening it with drops of rose and blobs of white, the streaky, uneven oval of paint on my palette took on an uncanny resemblance to my father's face.

I scraped it off and started over.

I bought a featherweight mobile, a colourful night light, soft facecloths, miniature slippers. I bought disposable diapers and tiny green nightgowns. I bought receiving blankets for ten times what I could sew them for—and sewed a dozen more in my head all the way home.

("You wasted your allowance on that? You can make doll clothes yourself."

"But it's cute."

"Unfinished edges. This stitching! It won't last a week.")

I sewed in my mind's eye in stores, cut and stitched each item of infant clothing as I felt its slipshod seams between my fingers.

My fingers worked roughly serged edges into smooth French seams, but only in imagination and desire.

I turned doorknobs with the machine in mind, the wheel I used to rotate to lift and lower the needle. I threw light switches slowly, as though dropping the pressure foot on fabric. I hummed the sound of sewing.

But I would not sew for my child. This I knew.

I had sewn for my wedding. I had sewn with my mother. No matter how poor the workmanship available at The Bay or at the specialty stores, I would not stitch this coming life to the one I'd left behind.

I would not visit my father.

I wielded my paintbrush as though it were a seam ripper, cutting ties.

Anticipation fired me with energy. I spent it in ways of colour and design, of planning and replanning. Ways that occupied my waking thoughts and most of my waking hours.

There were days when Kurt came home to no supper, neither on the table nor warming in the oven nor wrapped in the refrigerator. I became bold and restless, speaking my mind occasionally, acting on new wants and whims.

Kurt was not welcoming of the change in me. He was not resigned. He continued to drink and to stay out late, but he did not raise his hand nor, usually, his voice to me.

I see now that he was waiting.

15

Dear Asha,

I am settled now. My employer asks little of me: only to keep her alive a bit longer. This is easy.

I need only pick topics and pack her things, and keep my thoughts to myself.

After tending to Mrs. Oland's teeth and tea, I walk to the rectory. Perhaps Matthilda will sit with me as I clean; she does occasionally now. Sometimes she lets me be near her. But often she treats me as she ever did: slipping around corners, peeking while I vacuum or sweep, following me from room to room and rushing out when I turn to look at her.

Thanks to Harold, I've seen a new side to Matthilda.

He ate her apple with loud, crackling bites, then he twirled her in the kitchen, her eyes wide and delighted. He trotted down the hall when Patsy went out, Matthilda bouncing on his shoulder like a sack of potatoes. He tossed her in the air and caught her, and she squealed with terror and excitement.

I whispered to him, "It's so great how you get Matthilda to come out of her shell."

"Her shell?"

"Her shyness. How you make her laugh and, you know, really play."

"I do?"

"Well, yes. You just jump right in and . . ."

He looked confused. "Matthilda is shy?"

∽

The rectory's outside stairs are high, of dark green painted wood. I grip the handrail, a black painted pipe. The porch and the house feel solid but the rail is shaky.

Harold's a handyman; he could fix that. A hanging man, I'd like to say, for his hips are girded with hammer, drill, measuring tape, pockets of screws, and nails and plugs—hanging, as do his jeans: low, showing pasty flesh more grey than pink.

Father Jerome told me he's known Harold for a while. "He's a fixture here. Well, that is . . . He comes and goes."

I believe he sleeps at a shelter for men. He's dirty: hands, of course, and an odour that seems to leave him by midday. Perhaps it resides on the surface of his clothing, on the overcoat he wears outdoors even on very warm days. Perhaps it slides off when he enters the rectory, and I suck it up from the fringes of rugs as I vacuum. Perhaps when Harold returns to the shelter at night, the men smell incense and oil and a trace of Lemon Pledge, and think: *Harold the holy man.*

He has no claim to this place and no true place here, and so he is free to decode things, things that offer no sense to me.

I asked him last week, "Why is there no wheelchair ramp to the rectory?"

Harold nodded. "The stairs went in when the ground went up high like that, higher than the sidewalk. Then the priests wanted stairs."

I remembered telling Asha, "The wind blows the nests apart but the birds don't mind. The birds like to build." I told Harold I had a daughter, a daughter who is dead. I knew he would believe me and not ask to know more.

"She would have liked you," I said.

"Thank you. I would like her, too."

He knows nothing of motherhood, of tender bony shoulders soft with down, of little girls' toes and ribby sides that tickle under a washcloth in the bath, of the wonder of seeing how your own child thinks.

("Mommy, if I wasn't smart, would you tell me I'm not smart?")

Nothing of the pleasure of having wee arms encircle your neck on a sleepy morning. But perhaps, I think, Harold knows something of pain.

∞

Harold isn't here today. Father Jerome is out. I do laundry and organize the basement while Patsy works and Matthilda is at school. Before lunch I take a broom and dustpan up to the empty front bedroom.

It's not quite empty. A blanket has been tossed over two kitchen chairs and secured at the other end by windows, two of which are closed onto its corners. Someone must have helped Matthilda with that.

It's hot and stale with the windows closed. There are colouring books in the fort. I crawl in. *Dudley the Dragon.*

Playtime with the Care Bears. I choose *Santa's Little Helpers.*
I colour Rudolph.

"Marta?" calls Patsy.

"Upstairs."

Matthilda clomps up. Her footsteps creak into the room,
then stop.

"Hello," I call quietly.

Her knees appear. Then her hands. Her face. Her mouth
drops open.

I go back to my colouring.

Matthilda hesitates, then comes in. She peers at my page.
I shield it.

She gets on her hands and knees and climbs over my
outstretched legs. Her hair smells clean and fresh. She turns
her face and looks into my eyes.

"Marta," she says, "Rudolph's nose is not green."

When I get back to the bungalow, I tell Mrs. Oland about it—
about the colouring books and the way Matthilda watched me
after that, and how, when I opened the front door to leave at the
end of the afternoon, she came into the hall where she could
see me and almost said goodbye.

Mrs. Oland is still listening when I finish. "Yes?"

"That's all," I say.

She smirks: It isn't much of a story. "Little girls love
colouring books," she says. "Now you know."

Without a doubt, Mrs. Oland's most prized possession
is her photo of a dog, a dachshund she owned as a child.
She often holds the frame in her hands, at times without

looking at the image, just holding it close while she watches TV.

Only Mrs. Oland's feet are in the picture. Her brother is kneeling on the ground, arms around the dog. His smiling mouth is empty, shadows masking any hint of teeth. Mrs. Oland wears dark shoes with a double row of buttons on each. Her stockings are dark, too, her ankles as skinny as her skinny old limbs are now.

I nod toward the photo. "Tell me about your brother, Mrs. Oland."

She looks up. She has a funny way of wobbling her threadbare eyebrows. Not ha-ha funny. She looks surprised.

"I told him to let go of the dog," she says. "But he had to be the star of every picture. My brother. Ian. That's what he was like."

I hear what she is telling me. She is telling me *was*.

How can a single word mean so much, and in all ways different from its meaning before?

Everything is, now, before or after. Is or was.

16

I GAVE BIRTH in the local hospital. Kurt watched from against a wall, as though the enormity of my efforts had knocked him there and pinned him.

After long labouring hours, my daughter was guided out. She was separated from me, then she took my breast into her mouth and we were joined again.

I diapered Asha, her bottom shaped in two rounded hills, while she stuck toes into her little mouth.

I walked with her swaddled tight when she cried and hushed her with sing-song prayers when the scent of fever rose from her scalp like scalding milk.

Thoughts of my father wove into my disrupted nights and tired mornings, capsule images at the edges of my sleep. I regarded them dispassionately: there's Papa sitting at home, there's Papa stirring his coffee, there's Papa doing a crossword, scheming with Mama, lying to me . . .

The images exhausted me further, made me pull Asha closer.

I learned to spoon cereal past her toothless gums, and wept when the first sharp bit of white poked through, the first undeniable proof of her independence looming, gnawing relentlessly at my knuckle.

∽

Through the timeless first months, Kurt slept through the nights and woke heavily with the morning alarm. He showered and dressed in sullen silence, thickened lids hooding his eyes. He drank coffee and cleared his throat and drank some more. He put on sunglasses to head for the car, leaving me to hang his wet towels and wash the dark caffeine rings from his cup.

Women began to call me late at night, women like me, young mothers, young wives, women awake alone in compact houses. They called not to commiserate, but to blame.

One night I answered the phone and heard a woman's voice breaking. She pushed words from a throat stuttering with sobs. "Damn you and your husband. It's three in the morning, and Bill . . . He's out with Kurt again. He was fine before. A good husband. Good father. Now he comes home in vomit."

And I was tired, very tired. I murmured, "Now, now" into the handset, then as gently as possible I placed it in its cradle.

17

I WANT TO ASK MRS. OLAND about Patsy Wallace. I have a hard time seeing her whole, this woman whose every thought seems to be of her contributions to the parish. It is hard to believe that Matthilda is her child. Does Patsy understand what a fragile gift it is to have a child? Could she possibly be married, sleep nestled against a man, know the comfort of her own private fantasies?

I choose one easy question and pose it over our lunch of salty chicken noodle soup.

"I was wondering, what does Patsy Wallace's husband do? I've never heard her mention it, and I don't think I've seen him at church."

"You wouldn't have. He's not Catholic, believe it or not. Not anything, as far as I'm aware. Steven Wallace is his name. I shouldn't think she'd talk of him much. Her thoughts don't seem to be on him."

"On her husband?"

"As you've noticed. She has her ambitions and he has his. I suppose that's one way to make a marriage work, not that it was my way."

"What did your husband do?"

"Cold storage for furs. It was big business back then; he was run off his feet."

"You don't hear much of it now."

"Women don't get jobs to buy fur." She blows on her spoon. "He wouldn't have seen that coming. But it didn't matter. He went young."

"And Steven Wallace? What does he do?"

"Oh, he's a, you know, a consultant. He works out of their home."

We spoon our soup. It's bright yellow, came out of a box. Consultant . . . I catch myself beginning to wonder if that's something Kurt could do.

Mrs. Oland interrupts my thoughts. "Tell me, Marta, if you know: Why is it that a man with an office in his house is said to work out of his home, while a woman is invariably said to work *in* the home?"

I look at her with a stare so wide and surprised that she is herself startled. We ogle the whites of each other's eyes. Then she giggles, my eighty-eight-year-old budding feminist. Next thing I know, we're chuckling and guffawing—trying to hold our mouths closed, spluttering the table pad with scraps of soggy noodles.

I put a question to Harold when we find ourselves in the rectory basement on Wednesday: me, loading the washer, him, scooping drywall compound into a bucket and stirring in water, grey dust billowing around his hands. He's easy to talk to, though I can't pinpoint why.

"What do you think of Patsy Wallace? I mean, as a mother?"

"Good, I guess. She loves her."

"Patsy loves Matthilda?"

"Matthilda loves her mom."

"How can you tell?"

"You ever notice how she watches Mrs. Wallace? All day she's sneaking to the office to take peeks at her, making sure she's okay."

"But Patsy just shoos her away." I close the lid and lean against the washing machine. "It's so different from, well, my experience. They don't even seem to hug."

"Your mom was huggy?"

"I didn't mean my mother."

"It takes all kinds. Huggy or not. Anyway, you can't know about people. Not much point in wondering why they're one way or another."

∞

The rest of the week rolls by, bright early-May days.

On all my Sundays at Mrs. Oland's, some parishioner or other has pulled up unbidden at the front door when it was time to leave for church. It took a while for the word to go out that Mrs. Oland wanted the practice stopped.

Today I look out the front door and the coast is clear: We will make our own way.

I call for a cab. Mrs. Oland walks to the curb on my arm, slow but confident, and I help her into the car. When we pull up in front of St. Boniface, a four-block drive, a cluster of women disengage themselves from a larger group cooing in the sunshine. They come fluttering toward us.

"Mrs. Oland! We were worried you wouldn't make it."

"You know that Simon would be happy to pick you up! What kind of world is it if one person can't help another?"

"A taxi! Oh, I never! The young lady doesn't know to call us? Would we ever make you take a taxi?"

"On her pension!"

"Where's the sense in that?"

Mrs. Oland glows. "Oh yes, it's outrageous," she says, "the cost of taxis today. And the drivers prattle on. If I were younger . . ."

They take her arms, and I follow. Mrs. Oland's elbows point accusingly at me. The women sit with her in the front left pew, and I sit behind.

Later, they press envelopes upon her and slips of paper upon me, names and phone numbers printed large.

"Anytime," says one balding man, grey hairs poking from between the buttons of his golf shirt. He looks into my face and speaks slowly. "Mrs. Oland knows she can call me anytime."

We get a drive home, Mrs. Oland in the front.

"Thank God for friends," she says as I help her out of the car in her driveway.

I barely raise an eyebrow. Her forearm in my hand is like a chicken bone. Like a wishbone—but I've no one to snap it with.

∞

Mrs. Oland's son calls, and she answers.

"Oh yes, it's coming along," she says. "Much better now with Marta here. We work day and night; no rest for the wicked!" She smiles over at me, then frowns.

"Well, of course I'm kidding, Chester. Old ladies make funnies, too."

She listens. Her narrow nostrils flare delicately. "You haven't even met her."

I bring over a chair from the dining room, and Mrs. Oland sits.

"I told you, from the church. Patsy found her. The rectory administrator. You don't know Patsy Wallace?"

She lifts her hand in resignation. "What can I say, Chester? I need help, and Marta is help."

She shifts her body to face away from me. Her voice turns low and warbly. "I'll be careful. Does that satisfy you? Is that what you want to hear?"

The days are all the same. I roll a vase in four pages of newspaper and stuff the excess into its open mouth. I fold newsprint over the Pope's face on a commemorative plate. I crumple paper into balls and chuck the balls into boxes.

Mrs. Oland and I build a home of parcels around her.

Boxes stacked near the front door. Boxes half-packed in the living room, flaps spread like helicopter blades, waiting for the right item to fit into the remaining space. Boxes in Mrs. Oland's bedroom, under her bed, slid in so far you'd think she wanted to forget them.

Boxes fill the basement, their contents bound to disappoint.

When we wrap her few remaining possessions these days, I encourage her to stuff the newspaper into every cranny. It's exercise for her hands, wrists, and eyes. She often fails. But I praise her: "That's it, Mrs. Oland!"

I lay the objects carefully into boxes. I take the boxes downstairs. Then I unfurl the newspaper and, quiet as I can, wrap the items properly.

I ply my protective trade in reams of ink-saturated paper. I leave my fingerprints on everything, smeared.

This is what I send you, beloveds. Pull out the paper balls, unravel the sheets of newsprint, and see what is there: a mar, a mark.

I like to picture this: the ink on your hands as you dig through the box for more, the newspaper balls scattering across the floor.

I look at my blackened fingers and think: *messenger.*

"Mrs. Oland," I announce one day, "I have a brilliant idea. Why don't I take your address book and copy out the names in it. All your old friends. I'll put their names in a long list. Then we can run through it and write down exactly what you'd like to give to each person."

Mrs. Oland is sitting on the sofa with a Royal Doulton maiden on either side of her, draping each set of fragile china shoulders with a hand like a shawl.

"This is not a joke, Marta," she snaps.

"No, no. I just—"

"If you don't wish to assist me . . ."

"But I only—"

I stop myself. Mrs. Oland has begun to cry, quietly and furtively, with the Royal Doultons held in front of her face. I look away while she wipes her eyes with the backs of her hands. The figurines clink together.

"Never mind," she says with forced brightness. "I don't know why I keep that old address book anyway."

I grow flushed with sudden shame. So many people whom Mrs. Oland has collected through her life have shunned her or died.

She is not too old to care.

∽

That night I fall asleep like this: eyes forget they are closed. Nostrils fill with air. Mouth wets. A taste, a smell, a gentle volume of silver, its dimensions round in my mouth. Slow silver, beckoning, surrounding.

(*"Mommy, your words went in my ear and then they were in my mouth. That's how I heard them, Mommy."*

"Asha, my love.")

Awake, I pull blankets to my jaw, my body stiff with cold. I remember playing with mercury, rolling it in my palms. I imagine I am dying right this moment, dying from my memory of mercury rolling like a pill bug, rolling from lifeline to heart line to barely minted wrinkles in my young hand. I wonder where the mercury went: back into the glass vial held out to me by some other forgotten hand, splattered into an untold number of tiny, bouncing spheres on the table, on my legs, on a neighbour's linoleum floor, or silently settled into my pores, my growing cells, my greedy bloodstream.

I see my hands as stamp pads, fed with poison ink. I think of every apple I ever held. I wonder about streams and vessels and valves, and all the places in the heart where things can hide, and how some things are never washed away.

18

ON WEDNESDAYS AT THE RECTORY, I polish end tables, dust sacred knick-knacks, and mop hardwood floors. At times, a sound seems to be in the air, in the rhythm of running water, in the drone of the vacuum, in the rumble of the subway below my feet; I hear the thrum of a sewing machine.

I hear it as I stand at the basement sink today. Hot water fills my galvanized bucket, frothing and foaming as it blasts against cleaning fluid. An antiseptic smell heaves against my nostrils, smothering me for a moment: a sodden wool blanket pressed to my face.

The water is a heavy load to carry up two flights of stairs. This rainy Wednesday I am concentrating on its rhythm as it sloshes against the sides of the bucket. I don't notice at first that my grunting breaths are echoed from behind Father Jerome's door. The sound doesn't register until I've rapped once and swung the door open with my hip.

Father Jerome is lying on his back on a rickety bench halfway to the door, lifting weights. His expression as he stares at me is as rigid as the arms he holds straight above his head. His eyes and mouth are open wide. His arms begin to tremble.

"Inhale, Father," I say, dropping my bucket and moving

briskly toward his head. I guide the weighted bar to its stand, my hands between his, as he stares up the length of our arms. His abdomen is pale where his T-shirt has risen up. His sports socks are bright.

"You shouldn't lift weights in your socks, Father," I say. "You should have something with grip. It's not your arms doing the work. It's your whole body."

I sit on his tidy bed, clenching my fists and working my biceps.

"And you should start small, but with good equipment. What if this old bench were to collapse under you? Where on earth did you get such a thing? It's on its last legs. And the weight you've got there . . ." I shake my head. "The idea is to tax the muscles, tear and repair, a little at a time, not to exhaust them with a gargantuan effort. Determination is one thing, but . . ." I smile.

"How do you know?" Father Jerome finally asks. He is looking away.

"I learned all about it," I say, "where I came from."

He sits up on the bench and tugs at his T-shirt. "Germany? Kingston? Or wherever you really come from?" He glances at me. "That is . . . I'm sorry. I didn't mean to imply . . ."

"It's okay, Father." I smooth the bed covers beside me. "It doesn't matter."

"I don't need to know. Where you're from and all."

"All right."

"Only, you know, well, I *am* a priest. And if you, you know, ever want to talk . . ."

"You mean confession?"

"Oh. That's not for me to say, of course. The sacrament of reconciliation . . . I mean, it's there for everyone, isn't it?

All Catholics, that is, and . . . But of course. Confession. A wonderful sacrament. If you wish, whenever you wish."

I think about that. Father Jerome is nodding, nodding.

"My husband lifted weights," I say.

19

I'm PUSHING A RAG on the hallway floor when Patsy approaches softly.

"Marta?" Her voice is meek.

I look up but don't stand, so she crouches down beside me.

"There's a problem," she says. She steadies herself, fingers to floor.

I sit on a dry patch. She's never looked like this before, her eyes averting and voice unsure.

"I mean, I have a problem. I have a meeting, an important one. It just got changed to this afternoon."

I nod.

"People are coming in twenty minutes."

"You need me to watch Matthilda." My fingertips tingle as they dry.

Patsy says, "Can you give her a quick bite of something and take her out for an hour or so?"

My scalp tingles, too. I think of the places I could take her, how I'll take her hand in mine.

"Would you mind terribly, Marta? I haven't a clue where you can go in this rain."

"I'll figure it out," I say nonchalantly. "Call her and we'll go."

❧

In the subway, Matthilda gets six transfers from the automated dispenser. "I can make something with these," she says. "A little book."

I put them in my pocket for safekeeping.

We ride the train in silence. Each time a station is announced through the overhead speakers, Matthilda looks up at the garbled sounds.

"Next stop is ours," I say.

The department store has a big toy section and an abundance of noisy displays. Matthilda's eyes are large. I hold her hand and she grips my wrist with her other hand.

"Relax," I say. "We'll find you something good and get out of here."

Her head moves up, down, back and forth, scanning shelves and looking over at me, checking my expression.

"What's up, Matthilda?"

"Nothing," she whispers.

I barely hear her over the racket of beeping, chattering toys. My head begins to throb. "So pick something."

Her hand darts out and grabs a box. She hands it to me.

"Super Skateboard Sammy," I read.

She grimaces slightly.

"You want Super Skateboard Sammy?"

We stare at each other for a while. Then I put the box back and lead her down an aisle.

The toy department gives way to the nursery furniture area. It's quiet here among the cribs, all pastels and mobiles.

I sit on the edge of a display and take Matthilda onto my

lap. "What's up?"

"I don't want anything," she mutters, and her eyes grow moist.

"You don't want anything? Nothing? It's okay to not want anything. There's nothing wrong with that."

"I don't like all those toys. I'm sorry, Marta."

"It's fine. But maybe you'd like a T-shirt or a hairband? Maybe a craft kit?"

She wipes her eyes.

"Okay, then. Let's see what they have."

The craft supplies are in view at the end of the aisle when Matthilda stops.

"I want that," she says.

When I glance down to check the direction of her gaze, I'm struck by the intensity of her expression. I trace her pointing finger to the jigsaw puzzles.

"The one with cats," she says. "No, the one with boats. Please, Marta! The big one with boats."

"I didn't know you do jigsaw puzzles."

"My daddy does. I can't touch. I might lose a piece."

The puzzle pieces slide inside the box as I bring it down: a familiar, forgotten sound.

"My daughter's daddy did them, too," I say.

"You have a daughter?"

"She's gone now."

"Grown up?"

"Just gone."

"Just a secret now?"

"She is. She's our secret."

"We won't tell," says Matthilda. "So she won't go away again."

∞

Dear Asha,

If I speak of you, do I lose you in the words? Your name aches less sharply on my lips than in my heart.

And if I use the love you gave me, do I empty myself of you?

∞

Matthilda spends the rest of the day piecing together her puzzle. It is too large for her, and the pieces are too small. She doesn't care. She picks out all the matching colours and punctuates the floor in the front bedroom with piles of water, piles of horizon, piles of sailcloth, and edges.

Scatterings of joined pieces in couples and trios spread across the floor. She sits among them surveying her kingdom. When I come to the door, she ignores me, absorbed by her little world, by her immense and immeasurable challenge.

I'm changing Father Jerome's bedsheets at the end of the afternoon when Patsy comes upstairs calling, "Matthilda, it's time to go home."

Patsy marches toward the front room and I follow.

I expect a *Thanks* from Matthilda, perhaps even a hug and a *This was the best day*. Instead, I find her blocking the bedroom door, her hands and feet spread to the frame, her limbs an X.

"Don't touch my puzzle," she says to Patsy. "It's not finished."

Patsy stops. Her voice is quiet, controlled. "You're saying 'don't' to Mommy?" She turns and looks at me, suspicion in her eyes.

Matthilda drops her arms and takes her mother's hand. "It's my puzzle," she says calmly. "Marta gave it to me and it's mine."

20

MRS. OLAND COMES INTO THE DINING ROOM on Saturday morning in a slim suit jacket I've never seen before. It is of mauve silk with covered buttons, padded shoulders, and a generous sprinkling of cat hair. It's of a different class than the stretchy navy slacks she wears most days, including today.

I set down her tea. "You look nice."

"Thank you."

"Going somewhere special?"

"Not at all. Oh, this. I guess I haven't worn it in a while."

"Not since I've been here. It's a bit warm in the house for a jacket these days."

"Is it too warm, do you think? Shall I take it off?" She takes hold of the lapels.

"Leave it, Mrs. Oland. It's fine. There's just some—cat hair, I think."

"Oh my, of course. Help me take this thing off, won't you? I can't wear it with—"

"It's lovely. Leave it on and I'll pick the fur off with some tape. Just a sec. I'll—"

"Will you please just take this off me, Marta? I can't go around like this. Cat hair. It's been ages since I had a cat."

118

"But who's to see it, anyway?"

"Who! Who's to see, who's to know? For shame. Let me never hear you say those words again, Marta. There is always one who sees and knows. Between the Lord and oneself, there are two."

∽

I sit in the confessional, inhaling the scent of the varnished walls that shelter me. This is the only place I can speak of my past, give words to my guilt. I offer it in exchange for the penance that issues from the mouth of Father Jerome behind the veil of double screening in the window he never looks through.

He begins with a sigh. "Marta, don't think that I want to send you away. I am always happy to hear your confession."

I wait.

"But you always make the same confession and I give you the same answer."

"I do the penance, Father."

"But you don't need to do it over and over. Your penance absolves you. The sin perpetuated months or a year or many years ago does not return."

"But it doesn't go away, either."

"Marta, our Lord forgives you. I forgive you in His name. Be assured. Please. Do the penance this one last time, if you wish, and let yourself be washed clean."

"Three Hail Marys?"

He sighs again. "Three Hail Marys."

"Go ahead then, Father, please."

"I absolve you in the name of the Father and of the Son . . ."

Once there was a child born. She was born to me. She was naked for only a moment. I warmed her. I watched her. I wondered at her. And I named her.

I named her Asha.

Once a small, small child was born, and I cried with the shock of maternal love, and the name slipped out in a breath of surprise.

Asha.

Asha: a word sweet on the lips. I named her with a brush of her whisper-soft eyelids.

I named her Asha, and five years later she died in flames. How is this possible? How could my daughter be named Asha and be killed by fire?

By Kurt. Kurt: a name so blunt. Did his mother see her bloodied infant son and think of axe blows, a hammer swung, a thing destroyed? Did she deliver him to brutality with his christening, his name hacked out like phlegm—Kurt—short and sharp and final? (Like the words I gave him six years ago: "I do.")

Burn. Sear, melt, broil. Can you go through life, as a woman, without these words? Can you excise them from your vocabulary, extricate them from your memory? Bury them and believe they will not rise every night to flicker and dance in dark dreams, to roar in your ears? Simmer and heat and cook and flame and scald.

Ashes.

If only I had thought.

21

HAROLD IS KNEELING at Mrs. Oland's sink. He has come as
a favour to me, with his tools and his easy smile.

Even Mrs. Oland seems taken with him, despite his faint,
unpleasant smell, and despite her outburst when I told her he'd
be arriving.

"This is my house, Marta, and—"

"I know, Mrs. Oland. But your sink doesn't drain."

I brought Harold in and introduced him: "The handyman
from the rectory."

Mrs. Oland's face was closed as she approached, but she
met Harold's eyes and her posture relaxed. "Don't you look
like my Chester. My son, the one who lives in Perth. I don't
suppose you know him?" She smiled. "Well, you go ahead
then; I'll stay out of your way."

Standing behind Harold, I watch as he peers at the black
plastic pipes. He raises a hand and rubs his ear. I wonder
what's frustrating him but can see nothing. My gaze drops to
his shoes.

I think of bridegrooms with grease-penciled sos messages
scrawled on their soles. I think of little girls dressed like
angels, dressed like brides, kneeling with throats open to

receive their first Holy Communion, white patent leather pressed to red carpet, unscuffed soles directed at heaven.

Harold's shoes have thick bottoms that are flattened and worn on the outer edges. They take him through life precipitously, I think, as if he is ever straddling a peak. The worn leather uppers bulge at the sides.

I picture myself reaching above his grey-sweated socks, past the red stripes, slipping my hand up an olive trouser leg. My fingertips encountering dry, rough skin peppered with brown hairs. The calf bulbous, the knee boxy.

I retreat to the exterior of the sagging work pants. I follow them up past the rounded hips, noting the black belt hitched higher than the tan tool belt, its leather as overextended as the shoes. Above it, an expanse of white skin dips and slopes. Harold's hairless lower back is stretched taut.

In my mind's eye, I press my palm to the bleached skin in the hollow of his back, and my fingers register the silk of gentle blond fuzz: the invisible hair of a newborn child.

Suddenly I feel Asha's head in the cup of my hand, her mouth on the fountain of my breast. Memory jolts my body and I gasp with desire.

Something swells my breasts. Pricked with current, they tingle in anticipation. I tremble. My whole body bends to nourish, to feel the rush of warmth descend.

Then, as quickly as I feel it, the sensation flees. The promise is wrenched away.

I set a hand on the kitchen counter. I close my eyes and mask them with my palm.

I ache, but there is one small, mighty comfort: At least this pain is mine. Mine and not Asha's. At least I lived long enough for my daughter to have known me, to have had a mother in her life, to have been the first to leave. At least I lost her; she never lost me.

At least.

Perhaps this flow is only sorrow lancing my veins. Harold huddles near my feet. Something has sprung a leak.

22

WHEN WINTER CAME TO RESTIVE, the town with its snow-pitched roofs and voice-sapping cold reminded me again and again of Kingston.

I had settled into motherhood in my little home, had let my child's trusting eyes buoy me through each day, but as winter returned my mind strayed, catching on the hooks of my past. Standing at the window, at the fridge, pouring water from a kettle, ironing shirts, swinging slowly in the snowy park with Asha clutched against my chest under my coat, I thought about my father, alone with his paperwork in the long stretches between house painting jobs.

I was incapable of visiting him. His odd, quiet ways, his links to my mother, could draw me into her influence, could awaken in me her dissatisfaction.

The change from mother to not-mother had been sudden for her. Had she opened her mind to the possibility of letting go, of going, and felt the bonds fall away? Was that how it happened, just like that? Perhaps her restlessness was a trait lying dormant in my genes, waiting to be triggered.

I held Asha tight to me.

Nothing, no one, would separate us. I would never let her go. I would never go.

I pulled my coat tight around her. I would have pulled my skin over her.

∽

The first few years with my daughter were precious, holy, unforgettable—but they were soon overshadowed by the young Asha who walked beside me, whose mind was growing and wondering and noticing, whose heart at four years of age was big enough already to console and reassure me, and to bind me in knots of love.

Asha and I talked all day.

"Why do people ask me what I'm going to be when I grow up? Can't I be something before I grow up?"

∽

In the summer before Asha started kindergarten, on a night of thick August heat, Kurt drove onto a lawn. I fell against him in the front seat as the car bumped angrily over the curb and knocked down a stubby wooden fence.

We had left a party at Kurt's co-worker's house and driven semi-lost along rural roads.

Asha had said, "Daddy, are you in our lane? Because it looks like maybe you're a little bit not in our lane."

"I'm in the lane. For God's frigging sake! I'm in the lane."

He kept driving toward Restive until the curb came, and the fence, and the lawn.

Then I drove home with Kurt beside me and Asha in the back.

"Eenie meenie maka raka, era domma somma naka," Asha chanted. She rubbed the back of Kurt's seat with her sneakered foot as gently as she might stroke his hair. "Start with eenie meenie, Daddy. Come on, Daddy! Eenie meenie."

"Eenie meenie."

"Maka raka."

"Oh fuck." He threw his head between his knees and retched.

"Maka raka, Daddy. It's okay. You're doing good. Daddy? Maka raka . . ."

The streetlights reached down and pulled our car along. One by one, they speared the hood with a gleaming needle of light and pulled us forward, handing the car to the next lamp, and the next, and so forth. Not once did they fail to relay us, not once along the roads to Restive.

Asha's hours away in kindergarten were never a relief to me. I passed them in frenzied bouts of cleaning and impatience. I sat in the kitchen picturing her in class. Each day, before the time for putting on my jacket and heading over to pick her up, I stood at the door ready—early and eager.

My daughter and I discussed the world with a steady, inquisitive seriousness that my adult friends had never shown. But at home, when Kurt was there, by unspoken agreement we were quiet. Asha and I remained gloriously, conspiratorially silent while Kurt filled our home with cautious greetings, sullen mutterings, sloppy tears, or rage.

Home drunk late at night, lying prone on our bed: "Aaasha! Come take off my socks!"

On a bright morning: "Close the curtains. What do you want everyone looking in for?"

And on the day he forgot Asha's fifth birthday, sobbing, sitting on the sofa with his knuckles in his eyes: "I'll be a better father. I'll be good to you. No more drinking. No more."

"Hush," I said, alarmed at the flicker of hope I felt.

"Things'll be different."

"Okay."

"I'll stop. Really."

"Okay, Kurt. Stop then."

"You don't believe me. Don't lie to me."

"For God's sake."

"You think you can do better? Go whore for better."

"Go to bed."

"I'm not drunk!"

"You are. Go to bed."

He wiped his face with his sleeve. "Right." He stood up.

I hissed as he weaved away from me.

He turned, unsteady. "I'm sorry." Already he couldn't say the words with feeling.

Despite the sounds Kurt spat out, quiet descended everywhere. Sometimes, as Kurt yelled or seethed, my eyes would find Asha's. I would wink slowly, and she would squeeze her face into a like attempt. Then it was the most quiet. My ears, my mind, basked in inertia. I was wood. I heard nothing.

My heart belonged to Asha.

She was living. She had a life. She noticed springtime coming. She sang on the sidewalk in summer. She persuaded the rain to go away.

I let myself think she was immune. I gloried in it and was proud.

Then one day, in the midst of a slur of accusations, Kurt pronounced Asha's name slowly, with intention in his voice, and my ears opened. My eyes flew to hers, too late. Already Asha's eyes were locked on her father. He kept spinning words, speaking to Asha's upturned face, slipping promises in.

I understood then. Our raft of silence was vulnerable. There was no lasting safety in our home. To stay in that house with Kurt would be to take Asha by the ankle and pull her into numbness. Numbness, or worse.

I vowed silently: When the way opened before us, we would take it. I would flee like a sleepwalker, one foot in front of the other, with my daughter as my guide.

23

School began again, senior kindergarten. Asha was learning to read. She played with her friends in the classroom and schoolyard. At home she was mine and I was hers. Nothing could intrude; nothing would come between us.

"This girl in my class wants to come for a play-over, but I said she can't."

"That's good. Good girl. It's better with just the two of us, right?"

"I guess. When can she come over, Mommy?"

By mid-October the leaves had turned, but the weather was suddenly scorching. I bought Halloween candy and ate it in my kitchen. I thought about a costume for Asha, something light for the late heat wave, something I could buy without grimacing at the quality.

Kurt came home for dinner on a Friday and drank quietly at home on Saturday. He watched TV and spoke to me in easy tones of our small back lawn and the tiny oak sapling that had sprung up beside the shed. Would its roots be a problem if we let it thrive?

On Sunday he rose earlier than usual. His morning cough racked him all the way to the breakfast table, but he was awake and alert.

Sitting in the kitchen with fried eggs still coating his teeth, he pulled Asha toward him as she passed with a plate to scrape.

He spoke in her ear, cajoling. "We're doing something special today, Asha, you and me. We're going to a big park with woods and a lake. For a picnic. Go get pants in case it gets cold later."

I was coaxing dishes out of a sink full of near-scalding water, through a thick mantle of suds. My hands were red. I moved the dishcloth around and around the same plate, my movement slowing.

"You're going on a picnic?" I asked as evenly as I could.

Kurt took a swallow of coffee.

"Where are you going, then?"

He didn't reply.

"But why a picnic? Why now? You never take her anywhere!"

He reached toward the radio, turned it on, and fiddled for the traffic and weather reports.

Blood rushed to my face. I had to get him talking. I had to get him started, get him to speak. I scrubbed the plate. The dishcloth flicked hot droplets at me.

The splashing sounds were a mocking accompaniment to the clots of air that were catching in my throat. I squeezed normal words around them.

"What do you think: Is it better to fill the sink or to wash the dishes under the tap? Which do you think uses less hot water?"

He looked up, startled, then laughed.

Kurt waited outside with Asha, and a case of beer, for a tanned, almost-blonde woman to stop haltingly in front of our house. Two preteen sons were slumped in the back seat.

He stepped forward abruptly, pulling Asha.

Her head snapped toward me. "We're going to a picnic, Mommy. Okay?" Her body jerking toward the car.

The driver peered, and I stepped back into the shadow of the front hall. They drove away, Asha turning beside the two boys: no seat belts, no joy. I blinked into our empty street.

I spent too long digging in a drawer for a photo of Kurt. Asha would want to remember, one day. I put it in an envelope with my credit card, then pinned the envelope to the lining of my jacket.

I squeezed oil over the hinges of the front door and plied them into silence. Even drunk and sleeping heavily, Kurt had instincts like a junkyard dog's—not to protect, to fight.

Leaving everything else untouched, I drove to Restive's new bus station. We would go to Toronto, my daughter and I. Toronto was only an hour away, but it contained worlds. It held the possible.

The clerk handed me a schedule.

Monday to Saturday, buses departed on the hour. Ours would be one of them.

I bought two tickets, one way. "Do they have an expiry date?"

"Use 'em within six months. After that, you're outa luck."

I clutched them like lottery tickets, like a fistful of dice.

∾

Asha came home sun-tired and cranky with grass stains on her bare knees.

"I'm thirsty," she said.

When I returned with water, she was asleep on the couch.

"How was the picnic?" I asked Kurt. I poured the water into the sink.

"Sweet." He puckered his lips as if to whistle. His lean cheeks expanded and a boozy belch exploded out. His forehead and nose were bright pink.

"Did Asha have a good time?"

"Yeah. The best."

"How about your lady friend?"

"Friendly." He tipped his drooping face toward me. "Get a life, Marta."

"Look who's talking."

"I got more than a life. I got my little girl and my little wife—"

"And your little job?"

"My little goddamn job and my goddamn mortgage and two frigging sulky silent women at me every time I come home. You and your brainwashed daughter, like two frigging preachers."

"You should know better than to get drunk when you take her out. I didn't think I had to tell you that."

"You didn't. No. You're right. You got Asha to tell me instead. Every frigging beer. 'Don't drink too much, Daddy, how many is that, Daddy, are you going to drive?'"

"She knows right from wrong."

"Don't be so high-and-mighty sure." He smirked. "I gave her some beer. She really liked it."

"*What?* Are you goddamned stupid?"

"I'm a moron. But you know what? I'm her father. I can make decisions about her, too. Nothing wrong with giving a kid something to quiet them down."

I hurried to the couch and touched Asha's face. She seemed to be sleeping normally, her mouth open and moist. I smelled Kurt coming closer.

He dropped onto the sofa at Asha's feet. "They used to do that with babies. Put the pacifier in whisky or whatever. Better than—"

In one motion, I rose and slapped him. His stubble burned my hand and his drool drew across my knuckles and dropped, but his face barely moved. His eyes sharpened.

"She's my daughter," he said. "Get used to it."

∞

"Morning, Asha."

"Hi."

"How was the picnic?"

"It was okay. It was fun. I had two Popsicles. How come you never take me on a picnic, Mommy?"

∞

The next morning Kurt walked out the door and I almost left in his wake. I reached for Asha then stopped myself, lips dry, guts clenching.

I had to plan and prepare.

The task seemed enormous. I didn't know where to start. How does one leave, if not on the spur of a moment?

It was weeks before I realized that there was very little to it. Tickets, credit card, the photo of Kurt. What more could we need?

I packed a small bag of clothes, then rushed to return them to their drawers, terrified to see evidence of my intentions, a clue.

24

"MRS. OLAND! Mrs. Oland?"

I shopped at the drugstore and grocery store after confession and have returned to find the bungalow empty. Mrs. Oland is not in the living room, not in the sun-baked backyard. She is not in her high, iron bed nor collapsed in a bathroom. There is no note anywhere to indicate she's gone out—and where would she have gone? How would she have gone? Would a friend have phoned, arrived, and taken her away in the space of my two-hour absence, not even jotting a message or leaving a phone number?

I stalk from room to room, re-entering rooms, calling her name until it begins to sound as though it means something else altogether. "Mississ-so-land . . ."

I reach for the phone, but frustration stays my hand. Isn't there anyone who can help me?

Then I hear a quiet moan, a murmur. The sound comes from Mrs. Oland's bedroom. I spring toward it, fear rising in my throat.

Thin grey strands of hair poke out from the shadows beneath Mrs. Oland's bed. She twists her face toward me.

"Good Lord, get me out, Marta. I've rolled under again."

I'm flabbergasted, confused. Mrs. Oland is under her bed. She is not the least bit surprised.

"Stop gawking and lend a hand, girl. Can't you see I'm under the bed?"

I rush over to help. "But why are you? What happened?"

She groans again as I attempt to pull her out. "Gently, please, Marta! I just do this. That's all. I sometimes lie down for a nap on my bed and wake up under it. I've always done it. No one knows why."

I blink dumbly. We struggle together to get her onto her feet, then we sit side by side on her bed.

"Though I must say it's been a long while since it's happened. I believe the family thinks it stopped long ago. You won't tell them, Marta. You won't, will you?"

I shake my head. I won't tell them anything.

"Good girl. Now if you don't mind, my dear, if you look, you'll find my pillow under there."

I stay for a few moments with Mrs. Oland, then leave her alone.

I put her change on the dining room table in the small decorative bowl we use, without comment, for transferring money.

Money plays no official part in our room-and-board arrangement, but occasionally I ask Mrs. Oland what she needs, and she slips some bills into the bowl. I empty it to keep the supplies up. I don't mind shopping; I need to get out of this house now and then. I don't mind cooking; I need to eat. I don't even mind cleaning: Despite my weekly duties at the rectory, I find the minor upkeep of Mrs. Oland's bungalow neither tiring nor invasive. When the house is quiet and my body feels the need to keep moving, I'm glad for a distracting afternoon of sweeping, washing dishes, polishing wood.

I empty my bundle buggy and unpack the shopping bags, putting away all the items except a bottle of furniture oil. It is something Mrs. Oland has never requested. I bought it today because her teak bookshelf is drying out.

The bookshelf, though old itself, looks glaringly modern in the gracefully time-warped living room. One of her friends brought it to the bungalow when his den was redecorated. It's obvious that the teak hasn't been treated in ages. If I oil the piece now, it will absorb what it needs and let me rub the excess away. There was teakwood in my parents' small house in Kingston. I saw my mother oil it; this is the brand she bought.

I dig into the stash of rags under the sink and pull out the softest one. It's an old cloth diaper. It will work.

Quietly I pull the remaining books off the shelves and set them in piles on the floor. Mrs. Oland is lying down again, direct from her nap. Finding oneself under a bed is tiring.

I remove a dusty bundle of dried-out palm leaves from the top of the bookshelf. Palm Sunday palm leaves. What am I to do with them? At church they burn the leftovers and mark parishioners' foreheads with the blessed ashes of the blessed leaves before the next Easter. In my childhood home, we stuck our palm leaves behind the corners of picture frames, springtime green flags crisping to sharp-edged swords, the dry fronds shaping diagonal blond gestures along the wall. I wonder what my mother did with the leaves, eventually.

Is it forbidden to throw them out? It will be a question for Mrs. Oland. If she says to toss them back on top of the bookshelf, that's what I'll do. Eventually someone else will deal with them. Neither she nor I can stay here forever.

When I open the teak oil, I nearly swoon. The smell is heady and rich. Pouring a small amount onto the rag, I am torn. I want to open the doors and windows and drive the odour out of the room. I want to dive into the liquid and let it overwhelm and inhabit me.

After the first few moments, the odour mellows. I kneel on the floor and commence rubbing. The oil slicks onto the wood then sinks in, disappearing into the thirsty depths. I keep moving, rubbing, pouring, and buffing, until the lowest shelf is done. The teak looks almost like new. I smile as I reach for the next shelf.

Mrs. Oland's footsteps approach. She puts her bony hand on my shoulder.

"How did you know?" Her voice is hollow.

"To treat the teak?"

She is looking past me. "Did my mother tell you?"

"Your mother?"

"If I had smelled it anywhere I would recognize it. But here, in my own home . . . I never thought it would come here."

"You mean the oil?"

"The oil? That smell, Marta, is that the oil?"

"It's the teak oil, Mrs. Oland. You see? For polishing the bookshelf."

She focuses on the bottle, on the rag. Her gaze seems to flatten out, as does her voice. "Furniture oil. Well."

She reaches for an armchair and bends into it shakily.

"What did you think it was?" I ask.

She raises a finger and points at nothing, then drops her hand and remains silent.

"I'll make you some tea," I say, but I don't get the chance to do so. Mrs. Oland's voice rises, louder than before.

"Of course, it was oil. The girl had been working in my grandmother's room. It was where we kept the carvings my father brought home from overseas."

"He travelled a lot?"

"He was in mining."

"Your father was a miner?"

"Don't be silly. He arranged financing for mining operations. A financier. Oh, yes, he travelled a lot. He brought home souvenirs from all over the world. And the girl. We had servants then, of course. He brought one of them home himself, a girl from Africa."

"The girl with the teak oil."

"As you say. There were things to polish and oil, always something. My grandmother's room was like a storeroom of objects."

I would like to get back to my project. Once you start oiling teak, you shouldn't stop. It's strenuous work. If you don't do it all in one push, you'll never get back to it. I glance at the single finished shelf, admiring its soft sheen.

"The girl was young," Mrs. Oland continues. "Older than me but young." She looks up, startled. "Do you realize, Marta, how old she would be now? Good Lord. I wonder how she spent her years after my mother found out. I wonder if she's even alive now." She shakes her head. "She's always been 'that young girl' to me."

"You think of her often?"

"No. No, I don't. I wonder why I've thought of her today."

"It was the teak oil. The smell."

Mrs. Oland's face hardens. "It was everywhere in the house one day, that smell. The girl had been polishing, using the oil. Her hair and her hands must have absorbed it."

"Like the wood."

"But *she* wasn't everywhere, you see, the girl wasn't. The servants didn't sleep in our part of the house. The girl did her polishing on her polishing days, then she retired to her quarters behind the house."

"And the smell?"

"My father carried it. It lingered in every room he entered." She fixes me with a steely look. "He didn't bring his souvenirs across the ocean reeking of that smell, and he never touched the carvings once he'd delivered them home.

"But he put his fingers on my cheek and the smell was there. It was on his coat and on his arms. He sent me to the five-and-dime, and it was on the pennies in my hand.

"When I came home, the girl was on the porch. If I'd known then, I would've slapped her hard and sent her away myself. But she made me wait with her while my parents had words in the house." Mrs. Oland's lips twist down. "We grew honeysuckle outside. But the air was heavy with the smell of that girl. *That* smell."

She wrinkles her small nose. "People didn't divorce then, of course. Not respectable people. Certainly not Catholics. But children know when things have changed."

"What happened to the girl?"

"Gone, immediately. And now? Who's to say? Likely long dead." She settles deeper into the old wingback chair. I

can hardly see her face from my angle. I pick up my rag and
glance toward her.

One elbow lifts and juts forward as she brings a hand to her
mouth. "The disgrace that young girl brought upon herself. I
hope it followed her into her grave."

I grip the bottle of furniture oil.

Mrs. Oland voice breaks. "I hope she's languishing in hell."

Burn, baby, burn.

I raise my cloth to the shelf.

The phone rings as I'm closing the bottle of oil.

"Oh," the caller says. "You're the German girl."

"Marta Fett."

"I know your name. This is Mrs. Yolanda Oland-Edgar."

"Pleased to meet you."

"I am calling to speak to my mother."

I hand Mrs. Oland the receiver and go outside.

I stand on the front porch, letting the warm air steal the scent
of teak oil from my skin.

I picture my little house in Restive, an hour's drive from
here. I picture it from the outside. The window, the window
box, the green decorative shutters and the white curtains, the
door. I know that inside it is cluttered, untouched. I don't go
there. I have brought with me nothing.

Yet the nothing intrudes.

25

Dear Asha,

*I count in blades of grass the days until I will be with you
again. I saw them down. In wide swaths they tumble, a great
number crossed out at once to make up for all the hours and
months already spent waiting. I water in trepidation, not
wishing for new shoots to grow but unable to let the earth
scorch or the grass wither.*

I finally head back into the bungalow, but thoughts of escape
are nipping at me.

Mrs. Oland is asleep in front of the television. I write a
note: *"Gone out for a while. Soup in jar, in fridge."*

I walk to the subway and take a westbound train. There are
lots of empty seats, but I stand against the closed doors and let
the train rock me between stations. My legs shift against its
force as we accelerate and slow. My mind drifts into a nameless place. All the best places are nameless.

Two voices rise over the din of travel. I scan the passengers.
The loud female voice belongs to a mother who is talking to
her little girl. The other voice is a young man's. He sits facing

me, smiling and speaking loudly to another man, whose voice does not reach me.

"You see?" says the mother angrily. "I told you to hold on tight."

"No kidding," says the man. "She told me she was going, but I thought she meant with me." He laughs.

The mother reaches into her bag. "What a mess. I am so sick of wiping your face. If I could—"

"It wouldn't even cross my mind. You wanna know why? There're lots more girls where she came from."

I close my eyes and imagine the two of them dangling like marionettes from the overhead handrails that run the length of the subway car—their mouths flapping, words bouncing out, their arms dancing—while the train's brakes screech and commuters step on or off, station by station, the audience heaving and withdrawing like an accordion.

I ride the subway out and back.

Back on the sidewalk, I stand on Danforth Avenue in front of the IGA, trying to decide if I should go in for a carton of milk. The automatic door opens to let out a woman pushing a stroller. I don't know her, but I notice her.

She pushes the stroller across the sidewalk, looking straight ahead, oblivious to the pedestrians swerving on either side.

As she manoeuvres the stroller off the curb, the front of it tips up. The stroller falls backwards from the weight of the shopping bags she has hung from its handles. Two small Nike sneakers point skyward. A glossy eggplant rolls into the gutter.

We right the stroller together while her son screams. I end up holding her bags, Doris's bags. I hold them and walk with her, not just along Danforth but back into the subway station as well.

"Here, let me . . . Are you sure?" she asks, but she keeps on talking, too. Talking and walking, and dropping an extra token in for me. I keep holding the bags so she can carry the stroller down the stairs—then the train is right there. She hurries onto it and I can only follow. The sound of her voice rises and falls, and the train rushes and slows, and she keeps talking and talking, and I keep looking and looking at her toddler son. His hair shines blond where it lies on his head, and flashes white at the delicate wisp-ends that curve up like wings. When we step into the low-angled sunshine at the next subway stop, the child cries, cranky, and Doris rushes me along the sidewalk to her home.

The first floor of Doris's house is wide open inside. Doris carries the boy upstairs, calling out introductions to her husband over the escalating wails. The boy's cries reverberate. An arc of sound spreads itself thin as he gives in to sleep.

I sit with Doris and her husband, Dennis, drinking ginger ale. Dennis and I watch and nod as Doris talks about the frustrations of motherhood. She chats on as she works in the open-concept kitchen. She brings out a tray of cheese and crackers.

"Do you have children?" Dennis asks lightly as Doris pulls her chair closer to the coffee table.

I face him with a fixed smile. It takes me a moment to speak.

"No," I say.

(*"Mommy, can I ask you a question?"*

"You can always ask me a question, Asha.")

"Not really," I say. I stop offering answers then, aware that the next one would be yes.

We both look at Doris, who talks around the cracker in her mouth, but now and again I see Dennis glance at me quizzically: at my mouth, my legs, my hands. Once I catch his eye, and I am surprised at the hunger within it.

I am surprised I can still recognize it.

Doris's talk ticks onward. Finally Dennis offers me a ride home. I take it. As I walk out the door, I turn to smile at Doris.

I feel the muscles in my face stretching, my heart rushing, my legs wobbling. What does Doris hear? Not my bland "Nice to have met you"—not when her husband is leading me to the driveway, to the family van, to a journey far away from her.

Or perhaps I'm deluding myself. Maybe I am making it up.

In fact, he drives me directly home, pulling in at Mrs. Oland's bungalow. Shadows in the evening breeze pass over the van like a slow slap, back and forth and again. He was in a hurry to get here, barely braking for stop signs, not speaking but turning to grin at me every few seconds, anticipating.

Now we are here. He reaches down and moves his seat back as far as it will go. Toe to heel, he pushes off his shoes and grins again. I kick off my Birkenstocks and bend one leg under the other. Dennis stretches his hand toward me, flips open the glove compartment and pulls out a pack of cigarettes.

"I don't really smoke," he says, "but on a night like tonight, there's something about it. Reminds me of my friend Stan's cottage when I was a kid. Fifteen. Smoking behind the bingo hall, out on a rock ledge cantilevered over the lake. Menthol, like these. Even stale like these. We used to hide them under an old sheet of plywood." He takes out a cigarette and hands me the pack.

"We'd be gone for hours, sitting and smoking. Sharing a smoke, usually. I had the gum." He smiles, gazing through the windshield. "Every night he'd spit another wad of Juicy Fruit into the neighbour's firepit on the way home. If he was going home."

"Where else would he be going?" I take out a cigarette and play it back and forth on my palm. I don't smoke either, but on a night like tonight . . . I raise my cigarette and Dennis passes his over. A ring of orange burns behind the ashen tip: a solar eclipse. I light up and swivel to face him, imagining our knees touching. They don't. Yet.

"Stan would head to wherever the action was. Around the point there were some older kids, a brother and sister and usually a few friends up for the summer. The parents went up on the weekends; they were just as bad as the kids. Stan used to go there to drink, get shit-faced."

"At fifteen?"

"Sure. Beer, dope. Half the time I'd go over to bring him home, no one was there. They'd be out cruising the back roads, drinking, smoking up. Sending Stan into the truck stop for munchies. Turns out he was shagging the girl, and one of the guys might have been getting it on with him, too."

Dennis isn't smiling now. He blows smoke at the windshield. "Stanley picked the wrong crowd. They almost killed him after the girl got pregnant. They ran him down with a pickup truck."

The smoke drifts slowly toward my open window and rolls out over itself, swirling into darkness. "How did he end up eventually?"

"Don't know. Last time I saw him we were seventeen. He pretended not to recognize me."

Dennis puts his arm out his window, his hand on the side mirror. Moonlight and porch light play on the hairs of his forearm. Night air enters gently, a soothing warmth on a soft breeze.

What is a night like this to a boy? A boy who walks dusty cottage roads while his friend plays grown-up with the local trash. A boy perched over a lake. A city boy shrugging off the city, feeling it slide off with the sweat of cottage summers.

This night I remember playing pool in the congested heart of Toronto the day after I married Kurt. Playing pool by myself, against myself, after Kurt walked out of our motel room in search of a bar and a drink. I played until the owner bought me a beer, made me sit outside with him on that warm autumn night, made me stop playing. Too late: The captions of my life had already been rapped into the mesh pockets which hung low like scrotal sacs. The memories had been lined up and sent sharply in appointed directions, had smacked into each other, had been racked for another person's game.

I want Dennis to screw me in the family van, to get deep inside me and leave his history there: spawn of south Ontario. I don't want to get it this way, in dribs and drabs, little ideas dropped into my ears, awkward childhood summers pulled into my lungs with the cool menthol. I want it rammed in where it can't get out.

This husband, this man, he could give it to me. This night, in a van smelling of popcorn and filtered cigarettes, under the waving branches of Mrs. Oland's crabapple tree, I want to be the Canadian teen sneaking smokes over Lake Erie, hanging out while my buddy grows up in some deadbeats' shack. I want to lie on my back under a sky clotted with stars and find the sound of waves in the silence. I want to be the one to rub denim with the horny guy from down the way, to undo the zipper and work the jeans down over slender boy-hips.

I kiss Dennis with his mouth full of smoke, and we grapple with awkward lust until we come to our senses and crush out our cigarettes. Then we squeeze between the seats and kneel pressed together by the sliding side door.

The light is dim here, but I can see him beginning to recall the day that created this night and the wife who sent him off into it. His hands under my sweatshirt hesitate. He draws away, touches his fingers to his hair, and begins to straighten his composure. Quickly I pull his pelvis against mine.

"Just this once," I beg. "Just once, Dennis, and I won't tell anyone, I promise."

He complies, thrusting with increasing enthusiasm that never quite sparks the peaks of passion I need. I twist and groan in frustration, cursing, in the end, the choice of vehicle.

His seed is in me now. Not so deep, not so rich. Not the product of mutual combustion, but of acquiescence. A sprinkle of hand-warmed water, not the voluminous Ontario lake I'd hoped to be submerged in.

No whitecaps, no pollution, no sand-stubbed cigarette butts. Just a dribble of pity to wet my cooling thighs.

∞

Winter came to Restive, and there we still were, Asha and I. And Kurt.

There were things to do. Laundry. Research. I couldn't take Asha out of school. How could we leave in the winter? How could we leave the upstairs hall looking so unfinished? I hadn't sponged the neutral tone over the mottled peach and teal. I held colour chips and paid for paint rollers, my mind hardly drifting to the bus tickets in my wallet.

I planned Christmas. Christmas came and went.

I got drunk on New Year's Eve.

Then, one night in early January, I lay sleeping fitfully, dreaming. I saw a bus leaving without me, Asha peering from its windows. I gaped and gasped. My mouth was huge, my vision framed by my mouth as though I'd swallowed my eyes. I surged into anger and fear.

Then I heard, through my weepy haze of dreams, the front door slam.

Kurt walked into the bedroom and stared at me. His eyes scraped my body like icy shards. My skin rose in peaks. I could feel the roots of my hair lifting up. I could see everything. Everything was pulling me up into that night, up into the blackness.

I could see Kurt twisting inside, and I revelled in the sight.

As he approached, I rose to kneel on the bed. I reached for his buttons, his buckle and zipper, baring skin everywhere as his wary eyes followed my movements. Naked, he was all but powerless. It had always been so.

I spread my fingers on the curve of his belly. I made a map of his vulnerability: the open wound of his navel, the stitches of hair over the butter-skin of his nipples, the smooth rinks tucked up against his hipbones. I pressed my fingers in, marking him, mapping a sign language of disdain.

Kurt's body drowned into my touch. I pulled him onto the bed with the lightest pressure of my fingertips. I held him there, held him under me, below me. I held him down and let him stroke himself against me, but not into me. He reached for me, my hips, ribs, swollen breasts, moist bridges of armpits, sensitized spine. I held him back, below me, as my wetness slicked over him and he pressed to enter me.

He ached to fill me, to implode my pleasure, to make the night end.

I denied him.

I swayed panting above him, my breath breaking. Then my body cried open and I let him go.

He whimpered under me. I soared, triumphant.

But the seed Kurt hammered into me pulsed out a warning: *I. Will. Win.*

26

IT'S HUMID FOR JUNE. The city's cicadas are humming.

Sluggishly I mop the rectory kitchen, slowed down by the thick air and thoughts of last night with Dennis. At noon I set out sandwiches and plod upstairs.

Matthilda's doll is propped against a window in the stuffy craft room, its hair damp and warm in the sunshine.

I lay it down and pull the window open. "Did you give her a shampoo?"

Matthilda rolls her eyes. "My mommy did."

"Why?"

"You know. She wants me to play with it."

"So she washed it?"

"It was mucky. It was in our garden."

"You have a garden at home?"

She nods. "It's big. You want to see it? There's tons of flowers. There's a tree house, too."

"You have a tree house?" My voice is hollow, my chest feels cored. *You have a home at home?*

Matthilda looks at me and the enthusiasm drops out of her eyes. She slides the doll off the windowsill and twists its hair. "It's just that my uncle built the tree house. And the garden isn't so great. We could have a garden here if you want. We could make it together."

I shrug.

Matthilda's fingers twist and twist.

When I return from the rectory and grocery shopping, I am tired. I stand slouching on the sidewalk in front of the bungalow. The front door is too far. Between it and me there is grass and the shedding crabapple tree. There is a trio of juniper bushes. There are yellow tulips with fallen petals. Other perennials have come and gone, or lie waiting in the earth.

I put my bags down. It has been a long time since I sat on a sidewalk. A long, long time.

When I finally rouse myself, I enter the house to find Mrs. Oland running cold water on her arm in the kitchen.

She shows me her wrist. The skin is red. So are her eyes.

"I boiled some eggs," she says while I take her arm in my hand. "When they were done, I was bringing the pot to the sink and I tripped. I didn't fall but the water splashed out."

I glance down. The floor mat by the sink lies disturbed, at an angle. I take a close look at her wrist. "It doesn't seem too bad," I say. "You were right to get it into cold water."

Her lip begins to quiver.

"You won't scar," I say.

Ridges of tears spring trembling to her lower lids.

"All right, all right." I can't keep the irritation out of my voice. I am tired, I want to say. But I put my arms around Mrs. Oland and gently draw her head to my shoulder.

Her face is wet and her body is all bones. I reach for a tissue from the box on the microwave. I hand it to her and she dabs her eyes. Then she moves away from me and walks unsteadily toward her bedroom.

Her body did not bend to mine, did not give an inch.

I sit on the sofa picturing her. She's gotten frailer over the course of my time with her. It's visible to someone who's looking for the signs.

It's frightening that I can see it, frightening that I watch for it as if it were an outcome I'd mixed and measured for, as if I'd hoped it were inevitable.

She's gotten weaker. Her doctor removed a small mole recently, but there's no cancer in her; I know it. Unless cancer is a kind of sadness that slackens the muscles around the eyes, that causes promises and possibilities to fall loose from a face, stripping it of everything but the darkness around the sockets.

I know what she's got. She's got a life that has ended too soon, and her skinny old body just keeps on going.

This is my life, too.

∽

The minutes pass as I sit in the living room doing nothing. Mrs. Oland is snoring.

The phone rings and I get up.

"Hello?"

"This is Yolanda Oland-Edgar. Put my mother on, please."

"I'm sorry, she's gone to bed."

An exasperated huff. "It is only seven o'clock. I would like to speak to my mother."

"Mrs. Oland-Edgar, really, she's asleep. I'm sorry. Is this an emergency?"

There is a pause. Then the taut voice arches. "Next you'll be asking me about the nature of my call."

I could do that. I'm not sure what to do. I put the phone down and take a breath. I pick the phone up. My ears are burning. "I could wake her up for you, and help her sit up and get out of bed, and help her walk to the phone. You might have a long wait."

"Don't you try to—"

"It's not easy for her, you know."

"Oh, don't tell me." Her voice is cutting. "You think you're the only one looking out for my mother."

I hope not, I think; but maybe she's right.

I hear her exhale hard through her nostrils. Then: "You're not fooling anyone, Marta. We know what you are."

"And what's that?" I ask with some curiosity. Even I don't know.

"What would you call someone who has sex in an old woman's driveway?"

The phone line falls silent, except for a monotonous hum. It sounds like the middle place, the waiting place.

Then Yolanda speaks, triumphant. "Don't try to deny it. Lawrence told me all about it."

"Mrs.—" It is too much of an effort. "Yolanda," I say, "why are you calling?"

"What?"

"Why wouldn't you come over and break it to your mother in person?"

She snorts delicately. "You admit it, then."

"Admit what?"

"For God's sake! The sex, in the driveway, in the car!"

"What car?" I ask quietly.

"'What car'! It doesn't matter what car. It was a car and you were in it!"

"You're wrong," I say. "It was a van."

Her breath sucks in as I hang up the phone.

In bed, I rock slowly from side to side, tucking the blankets tight along the length of my body. My arms are crossed, my hands burrow into my armpits.

I try to imagine that I am Mrs. Oland, and she is me. I close my eyes to the shadows that shift on the ceiling; I do not want Mrs. Oland to lie awake with her bewildered eyes flicking here and there. I try to feel the lightness of her bones and the lifting of my own memories. I search for a way to care for the faces and years that parade past for her. I drift into a roll call of the items we have wrapped and boxed over the months, but when my head dips into the pillow, I start awake.

I see my home in Restive, with all the objects of my former life, just exactly as I left them on that March afternoon. They are crisply outlined and waiting.

What evidence did Kurt and Asha leave for me? No message on the kitchen table, no valuables missing, lipstick intact on the dresser, Barbie in her Barbie bed, nothing packed, nothing discovered, everything stabbed with familiarity.

Kurt's travel bag hung unused on the open closet door. I lifted it off its hook. I carried it with me like a security blanket. Where was he taking her? Had he intended to bring her back home?

The stairs held no clues. The walls of the basement were clean and unmarked, unpainted drywall taped at the seams, unfinished. Boxes of empty bottles, stacked. Laundry bins, full. The kitchen refrigerator fell silent. No note, no knives out of place, no pencil knocked to the floor. Living room spattered with Asha's artwork and kindergarten papers, hiding nothing. No answers, no receipts, white curtains hanging open. Two bedrooms.

I walked the house.

There was nothing to find in my home, nothing to look for. I haunted the front hall for days, for weeks, struggling to picture the departure. I imagined—a hundred ways—Kurt in the car and Asha crossing to him. Daughter crossing the sidewalk, father opening the door for his child. *"Hop in, we'll go to the library. Come with me to the store. To a park. To a picnic. To Disneyland. To—*

"Get the hell in the car I said now."

I remembered, rewrote, reconstructed, rejected the moment of receiving the news. *"Are you Marta Fett? Wife of . . . Mother of . . ."*

No, I should have said. *No, I am not. No.*

I slept on the living room couch listening for the front door. I slept at the bottom of the stairs to the second floor, my feet pigeon-toed on the linoleum. I slept on the floor in the front hall with my head on Kurt's duffle bag. I lay with my eyes open and dry. I sat awake all night, then slept at the kitchen table with my chin in my numb palm.

I waited for Asha to come home.

∾

Mrs. Oland and I settle ourselves at the dining room table in the morning.

"Yolanda called last night," I say.

"She did?" Mrs. Oland sits up straighter in her chair. I've never known anyone who can sit so straight.

"She said not to wake you," I lie.

"Not to wake me! Why would she call after bedtime and say not to wake me?"

"Maybe she doesn't know what time you go to bed."

"Well, she should."

"Of course she should."

Mrs. Oland's eyes narrow. "What do you mean by that?"

"By what?"

"'She should.' What are you implying?"

"Nothing. Only that a daughter might know a little about her mother's habits."

"Oh, should she? And how should she know such things? Yolanda does not live here."

"No."

"Well," says Mrs. Oland. "Well, then, whatever do you expect of her?"

"I don't expect anything. What do you expect?"

"I expect . . ." She pauses. Her eyes flutter down, the lashes hardly dark enough to shade them. Then they lift full of indignation. "I expect respect. For my daughter as well as for myself. Do you understand?"

I nod. "You expect respect. For your possessions, for your family, and for you."

"It seems to me you're having some difficulty with the idea."

"Not at all. I was a child once. I know all about respecting everyone, whether or not they deserve it."

"You act as though you're still a child: a spoiled child!"

"Oh, right. I've got everything I could ever want in life."

"It's not my fault that you ran away from everything."

Instantly, my body goes cold. My words are slow. "What do you mean, 'ran away'?"

"From Kingston. Up and left everything, at twenty-six, just when you should be settling down. If you were coming to a husband, or with a husband, I could understand. But to come with nothing? To nothing? Why on earth would you uproot yourself to come to nothing?"

The stiffness leaks from my limbs and my lungs. I even smile. "Oh, I might not come to nothing, you know. Someday I might make something of myself."

Mrs. Oland isn't amused. "You know what I mean, Marta. Don't think there aren't tales being told about you. If I weren't so trusting, you'd be on the street by now."

I'll be there soon enough, I think.

She says, "You never speak of yourself. You appear to have no interests, no family, no anything. What do you expect people to think?"

"It looks bad, doesn't it?"

"Yes, it does." She is appeased a little.

"I should do something about that."

"Well, yes, you should." She wiggles in her chair, ready to hear my story.

"Something like get a husband," I say. "Get some stuff."

She stares.

"Get my old life back. That would be a neat trick. Do you ever want your old life back, Mrs. Oland?"

She turns her face away.

I press on. "Tell you what. When I figure out how to get mine, I'll let you in on the secret."

"This is entirely inappropriate."

"We'll go back to the good old days."

"I said—"

"Love. Family. Things; can't forget our things."

"*Our* things?"

"You're right. Your things are all still here. It's come in handy, keeping them around. Gives you something in common with your children. Something to hold over them."

Mrs. Oland bites her lip.

All at once I stop myself. The end is near enough; why am I driven to pull it closer? "I'm sorry, Mrs. Oland. I don't know what I'm saying. I didn't mean that the way it sounded. Here, I'll make us a cup of—"

"No."

Her eyes flit across the dining room table. Her hand slides over to the dental floss. She curls her fingers around it. She's not going to let me near her.

∞

A few minutes later, I hear the garbage truck turn onto our street. I go to the front door.

The driver leans out the window, over his elbow that hangs out the window, while the brakes squeal and his partner leaps off the back of the truck. I lift my hand to the glass in a wave in case one of them glances my way.

In all these weeks, they've never looked at me. Yet it has cheered me each Thursday to see this dependable, efficient team that rumbles and hauls through the streets, collecting the secrets of our trash. I should've been a garbage collector, I think, instead of a . . . whatever it is I am now.

When they've passed Mrs. Oland's bungalow, I go out and bring the empty can to the house.

As I open the side door, I hear the telephone stop ringing in the kitchen.

Mrs. Oland says, "Hello?"

I move toward her, then freeze.

"Yes, Yolanda, I know. Of course I was asleep." Her fingers lift to her mouth at the phone. Her voice tightens. "What do you mean?

"What has happened? Just tell me, please.

"Then come right away. We'll be waiting for you. Please hurry."

She hangs up as I approach, and holds out her trembling hands.

"Yolanda is coming right over. Something awful has happened. She needs to tell me in person. Oh, Marta, I'm so worried. This isn't like her at all."

I lead Mrs. Oland to the dining room.

"Just sit for a minute," I say. "I'm sure it's nothing that terrible. And it'll be nice for you to see Yolanda, won't it?"

"She said she wants you to be here when she tells me. She must know I would need someone, that I would need you here with me." Tears swell in her eyes. "It must be serious. Yolanda is terribly ill, I know it."

"Mrs. Oland," I say, "I spoke with her last night. She's fine."

And because this will be my last chance, I put my arms around her. This time she rests her head on my shoulder. Her thin, rasping breaths quiver against my neck.

∽

Yolanda is not what I expected: not very tall or thin or rigidly straight. She has dyed red hair and her eyebrows are over-plucked. She could be any woman at the bank or supermarket, but for the silent derision with which she looks me over.

I brush past her, leaving her to make her own way in. As I do so, her eyes shift to the interior of the bungalow, and in that instant I glimpse insecurity in them. In them, I see Yolanda as a daughter, a daughter out of her element in her mother's home.

The back garden is beautiful now. Morning sunshine darts through the tops of the young asparagus ferns. The poppies have burst out early in red and orange. In a shady corner of the garden, our unconfined compost pile is sprouting lashes from the eyes of potatoes.

The flower beds are rimmed by long blocks of wood, as dark as old railroad ties. This is where I sit, low to the ground, my eyes on the grass. Each ragged-cut blade casts a ragged shadow.

I can't see either of the house's entrances from here.

I list mistakes as I sit in Mrs. Oland's yard. Mistakes of motherhood, of marriage, of youth. I hear my father's voice counting, and add him to the list. My failings stack up like Mrs. Oland's boxes. Who knew one person could have so many?

I list probabilities: I left the can in the wrong place on the shelf after oiling the hinges of the front door. Or Kurt watched my sleeping breath and read the tremolo fear that jugged my lungs. Or he sank his hand down the inner pocket of my jacket and found my two pairs of underwear coiled about Asha's panties and socks. That was all I would have needed to take. That, and the hope Asha gave me.

The rusty spring of the aluminum side door creaks.

My fingernails hook into the side seams of my jeans.

Yolanda's voice, argumentative, comes muffled.

"I said no," Mrs. Oland replies firmly. "I shall deal with it myself."

In a moment a car door slams and an engine veers away. Still the aluminum door has not squeaked shut.

I press my nails into my scalp, the heels of my hands into my eyes, and imagine Mrs. Oland standing in the doorway—disappointed in me? Shocked? Perhaps defiant. Loyal.

When I lift my head, she is careening over her cane, each step too long and too fast.

Her eyes look fevered as she approaches. Their intensity reaches me well before she passes the small storage shed and begins to weave her way across the grass. Finally she looks down on me with a twisted smile.

"So you thought you could deceive me."

The hairs on the back of my neck creep up. I pull my shoulder blades together. There's a shiver of electricity trapped in my scalp.

I keep my voice to a cautious monotone. "I don't think so, Mrs. Oland. What do you mean?"

"You go to church with me. You take me on your arm. The perfect picture of sanctity. You made me trust you, against all the warnings from my children and that . . . that snake, Lawrence. They told me about your kind. How you'd take advantage, sneak around. Do you realize I stood up to them? I told them you were quiet, perhaps a bit different, but you were a good girl."

Now a surge of anger straightens her spine and grips the knuckles over her cane handle. "And then I hear what you do when I'm asleep."

My heart pounds. "What do I do?"

Her mouth is tight around the words. "You shame me."

I push myself up off the wooden block. Standing up seems to go on and on.

∽

Shame: My child was Kurt's child, too. I dangled this in our last conversation when I called from a downtown phone.

"Can't you feed your own daughter, Kurt? Tide her over; I won't be long. After I get the paint chips, I need to go to the library."

"Don't bullshit me."

"I don't want to have to go out again tomorrow."

"Why not? Your boyfriend busy tomorrow?"

"I'm heading into Canadian Tire now. Make a box of mac and cheese. I'll call from the library; you can pick me up there."

"Hurry up. Asha's whining."

"Deal with it, Kurt. Okay?"

∽

"Mrs. Oland," I say, "if I've done something wrong—"

"Everything you've done has been a lie!" she hisses. Her thin lips cannot cover her teeth. Her teeth filter her words into spurts. There is saliva gathering in the corners where her trembling mouth turns down.

She raises her hand to me and pulls back to strike.

I am suddenly enormous with defeat and grief, deaf with vengeance, a freak of nature reaching for a very old woman, reaching in slow motion, very deliberately grasping her wrist. I stand rooted in my own strength, thrilling with the power of not breaking what is fragile.

She falls on cue, her mouth open and silent, the shape of *oh*.

Her eyes lock onto mine. They are frightened. They pull the anger away from me.

Her eyes deflate me.

Feeling again the exact shape and size of Marta, occupying no more space than I had before, I bend to help Mrs. Oland to her feet.

It is a tricky operation. Getting her back into the house will be awkward, too. Already I am embarrassed for her, for her frailty, for her reliance on me.

We inch our way across the lawn. Mrs. Oland is on my arm. She is calm, her anger exhausted. At the side door, she gives me a small, contrite smile.

Later I hear her on the phone, sounding years younger, almost spry: ". . . got my mettle up, I tell you!"

It must have been a while since she had a rip-roaring fight; it seems to have revived her spirits.

"Oh goodness, that would be sixty-odd years ago . . . Well, maybe I do remember . . . a nice lad named Charles." Her voice drops conspiratorially. "There were no vans then." And she giggles.

That night I scour my room for my belongings. I've not accumulated much in my time with Mrs. Oland. Everything fits in the duffle bag with space to spare.

I expect a sleepless night of weighing my options. Instead, I sleep like a rock.

In the morning, I make tea: black, one sugar. Mrs. Oland sits in the dining room, one skinny forearm on the table.

I pick up the container of dental floss and she opens her mouth, then closes it.

"Your young man," she says. "I'd like to meet him."

"I don't have a young man."

"But— It wasn't a young man in the van?"

"Not my young man."

"Then you didn't . . .?" Her fingers on the table fidget.

"You sound disappointed."

"No, no, of course not. It's just that Lawrence told Yolanda he was sure."

"And how would he know?"

"Perhaps he wouldn't. But he said he was in the shed, returning a gardening tool, when the van pulled into the driveway."

"He was in your shed?" I slowly wind the strand of dental floss around my fingers.

"Returning my clippers."

"You don't lend your clippers."

"Apparently that's why he didn't knock."

"Or park in the driveway."

"But there *was* a van, Marta?"

"A friend gave me a ride home."

"I knew it." Mrs. Oland shakes her head. "Lawrence goes too far. He did the same sort of busybody snooping in my family."

She pauses with a meaningful look.

"He thinks he's impressing Yolanda. Tracking down your father. Phoning us with nasty little reports, crazy stories, trying to sway me—as if I can't judge a character for myself."

The floss chokes the blood from my fingertips.

"Not that I pay any attention. I tell him every time, 'I can fend for myself.' You'd think you were an axe murderer, the way he harps on it."

I try to moisten my lips, but my tongue is dry. "On what?"

"Oh, you know: your secret past. I told him, 'Marta will tell all in good time. She's entitled to her privacy.'" She is pleased with herself. Her fingertips dance.

"Thank you, Mrs. Oland."

She gives a modest wave. "Not at all, Marta. We both know that Lawrence's claims involve more than a little imagination."

I lift the floss and Mrs. Oland opens her mouth automatically. I have done a good job these past months; the floss moves swiftly between her molars.

"His claims? Such as?" I ask quietly, rewrapping the thread around my fingers.

"Oh, saying you have a husband, for example. He was very worked up about the husband. Not that he had a shred of proof. Ask him for proof, and the husband disappears."

I floss around Mrs. Oland's eyetooth and don't meet her eyes. "Husbands sometimes do," I say.

"There are other examples. The child! Your child disappears, too. See what I mean?"

I hold the floss taut.

"Gone in a puff of smoke."

I pull the floss tight.

She laughs. "Easy come—"

I push it between her top front teeth. If I push hard enough, I will slice her in two.

Mrs. Oland bucks. Her hands fly to mine. Her eyes are wide and wild.

I extricate my fingers impatiently.

"All done!" I say brightly, briskly, and clap once.

A long strand dangles from Mrs. Oland's teeth.

("One little angel, all dressed in white, tried to get to heaven on the end of a kite . . .")

The indignity of it, the string hanging below those startled eyes. A small grin sneaks across my mouth and I cover it.

My fingers throb hot against my lips. Quickly I lift them off.

My fingertips are purple and indented all around.

I see what I've done.

I draw in all the air in that boxed-up room. And I crack into sobs.

My palms shake against my face. Tears pool between my fingers and rush trembling past my wrists.

Before the flames poured high into the winter sky, I stood choosing books on home decoration, knowing I'd be gone before the due date and planning to return them early to keep my record clean, clean as the colours I would whip onto the walls to change everything, everything I was going to leave behind.

Did I not believe I would leave it behind?

I stood smiling into a book, content that I would transform our house but forgetting for the moment our entangled hearts and lives, the lives that would ignite in a car on an on-ramp to the highway that I would not take with my daughter, would not escape on, that I would imagine every day pulsing with travellers while Asha and Kurt roared into blackness, smoke smearing the snow while gridlocked commuters swore.

I put my books on the counter and handed over my card and borrowed until all time ran out.

∞

"Asha? Why are you answering the phone? Where's Daddy?"

"Where are you, Mommy?"

"I'm still at the library. Can you and Daddy come pick me up now?"

"Daddy says you're somewhere else."

"What?"

"Someplace with someone. Lover something."

"Oh, my God. Put him on the phone, Asha."

"I love you, Mommy."

"Where's Daddy? Is he there?"

"He's out in the car. It's smelly from beers. I didn't want to sit with him any more."

"Okay, Asha. I'm coming home. Don't come get me."

"Daddy says he's going to get you."

"Don't let him, Asha. Please. Go out there and tell him not to drive. Tell him I said so."

∞

I cry for a long, dark time.

In the end, I raise my head. Mrs. Oland sits before me. She looks tired. There is no judgment in her eyes.

"Marta," she says in a voice gentler than I have ever heard from her, "I have arranged for your return to the rectory. Patsy is preparing your room."

"She wants me back?" My voice is scraped and raw.

"'Wants'? No. But it's going to be a long summer for her. She's full-time now, with the big fundraising drive, and Matthilda's school holidays are about to begin. She needs help. Not that she would admit such a thing, but she needs you back. It could be a good experience for you, being a nanny."

I smile weakly, not certain what I feel but believing in full faith that Mrs. Oland knows best.

"What about your parcels?"

"Lawrence will be by shortly. I'm sorry. I have no one else to ask. If you would accompany him to the post office with them, he will drop you at the rectory afterwards. Do take your bag."

The bag sits beside the sofa, its zipper slumping onto my rolled-up Sunday dress, my sweatpants, toothbrush, jacket, and a single change of daytime clothes. I fish out my key ring and detach Mrs. Oland's key. I place it in her hand like a letter, then drop the ring to the bottom of the bag, where it will rattle with me back to the rectory, back full circle.

27

I waited two months, alone in Restive.

Kurt's friends phoned. Police officers. Insurance representatives. Bank employees. Everything was taken care of. Casseroles came to the door in hands I didn't know. Hands led me places. People drove me. I signed things. I walked the house. I walked the winter. I ate. I waited.

No one came home.

Officer Crombie came. As a courtesy.

I didn't much remember Officer Crombie.

"That's understandable, ma'am." They would be closing the file. No point in dragging it on. The reports substantiated each other. Nothing was left unexplained.

"But you said yourself, Officer. You said they could have walked away from it."

"Mrs. Fett, I said *if* the explosion hadn't occurred. But hitting the guardrail at that rate of speed, at that angle . . . It's not hard to imagine how it happened. When the car flipped over, the gas tank would have caught right away."

"But before . . . before the gas tank, she could . . . she could have . . ."

"Mrs. Fett. Ma'am."

I saw him to the door.

I followed him out. In one hand I held the empty duffle bag, in the other, my keys. I locked the front door behind me.

What was I hoping to protect?

∞

In my wallet was Asha's bus ticket and my stub. I sat beside a window. The seat beside me was empty. My bag was empty. My hands. My lungs.

If the explosion.

"Are you Marta Fett. Wife of . . . Mother of. . ." No.

But I *was* Marta Fett, mother of.

Was.

Noose of three letters. A siren's call of loss. This was the beginning of *was*.

I knew there existed a time before this. I steered my mind toward it.

When I saw my daughter's eyes in my reflection in the bus window, I closed my own to the sight.

I imagined myself, little girl. Small, happy girl: a child in need of little. Playing silent on the floor behind my mother's sewing chair, buttons in piles around me. Favourites. Uglies. Blues, yellows, browns. Three fuchsia coat buttons as big and smooth as chestnuts. Sliding bumpy, creamy-white buttons along my upper lip, gripping their posts with just the tips of my fingers. Staring into tiers of plastic: tiny balls melted into careful layers, pretty as a wedding cake.

I called up a memory of my mother's arms around me, the cooling pressure of her hand on my fevered forehead. I recalled the even way she watched as I ate.

I remembered the story she told: how the tiger chased its tail around a banana tree, became a blur, became in the heat of the equator a streak of melted butter.

∞

Lawrence arrives in his silver sedan and idles in the driveway as I hug Mrs. Oland.

"I'll bring out the boxes," I tell him.

"First things first," he says. He leans across and opens the passenger door.

28

PATSY STEPS OUT of her office.

"Matthilda, come down!" she calls. It's a hot, humid day and Patsy's face is flushed, but her hands wring each other dry.

I've arrived to provide relief in her long mother-and-child summer, but relief isn't always welcome.

Before Matthilda's light footsteps reach the stairs, Patsy jabbers, "It isn't easy to find a nanny, not for this kind of placement: just for the summer, then down to half-time. And Matthilda's overly sensitive. She wouldn't even come into the room to meet the nannies I interviewed. At least she knows you."

"It'll be okay. Matthilda actually really likes me."

"Oh, please." Patsy rolls her eyes. "She does not attach herself to people."

Matthilda appears at the top of the stairs. Slowly she makes her way down, looking back and forth from her mother to me.

"Is it Wednesday?" she asks. Her left hand clamps onto Patsy's skirt.

"Marta is going to be here every day. She is your nanny now."

Matthilda's eyebrows go up. "Really?"

"Yup," I say. "I'll be the nanny goat, you can be the kid." I lean down to butt my head against hers.

Patsy puckers.

I ignore her. "That a deal, Matthilda?"

Matthilda doesn't answer, but she takes a step forward. Still clutching the side of her mother's skirt with her left hand, she reaches out with her right. Her fingers press against my jeans and dig up a small handful of fabric.

Her mother and I face each other across the bridge of Matthilda's arms.

Patsy says, "I am hiring you to supervise her, not to be her buddy or her mommy; Matthilda has those things already. And keep the rectory clean. I have no complaints about your work in that regard."

"Supervise and clean."

"Exactly. Not so different from your Wednesday duties, except that you will keep Matthilda from distracting me. You can have your old room back, and you'll be paid weekly. Does that suit you?"

"That's a deal," I say, and Matthilda looks up at me.

Patsy peels her daughter's fingers off her skirt and strides toward the office. "Set her up with a snack in the kitchen, please. Then come to my office. I'd like to have a word with you."

∾

Patsy waves me into a chair and leans forward, a woman with something to say, something helpful.

"I have one piece of advice for you, Marta. One day you'll thank me for it." She pushes her bangs off her damp forehead.

"Okay."

"I know your biological clock is ticking. Don't act surprised," she adds. "I recognize the signs. Your strong need for Matthilda's affection. Your indiscretions at Mrs. Oland's. I didn't have Matthilda until I was thirty; I know how you feel. I mean, I used to know. But then I got married. You see? You have to do these things in the right order."

Patsy's phone rings. Before she picks it up, she touches my arm. "Try to manage your urges. Put your mind to it; you can be a model of control."

∽

Matthilda and I hover around each other for the rest of the day. I let her help me make a pot of stew for the evening's supper, and then she and Patsy are gone for the weekend.

That night I wake in the blackness to the sound of my voice. In the corners of the ceiling, the smoke still lingers. The air swims like a mirage.

The bedroom door is ajar, and Father Jerome is framed there. I sense his hesitation, his embarrassment.

He has heard my confession. He does not consider it a sin to have let one's daughter burn to death. If I had left my husband, then I would have something valid to confess.

The door closes quietly.

I remain in fear of sleep, yet I sleep.

I dream that I am under Harold. His body is huge. His bulk blocks out all light like a bird covering an egg, and I fall silent and still, am nourished and pathetic.

When the very early morning comes, it brings shadows I remember from my early days here. I lie in bed for twenty long minutes. The tension in my gut grows. The minutes vanish for nothing. They cough up memories, and I fight a rising ripple of pity.

∾

Dear Asha,
    No one cries for Kurt.
    Must I?

29

MATTHILDA'S LAST SCHOOL WEEK passes in dishes and dusting, in construction paper crafts and games of hide-and-seek. Now she's here at the rectory all day—all day with me.

"That's my life now," I explain to Harold one evening, as he accepts a cup of coffee outside after rejoining sections of the house's downspout.

Harold says I have been chosen. "Chosen for the rectory. For your new life."

"I know." New life, big city life. Packing china, scrubbing counters, watching someone else's child. Life of loss. One day at a time life.

"Me too." He nods. "My life is new every day. I got chosen, too."

We smile. I feel a sharp rush of actual happiness, and step down two stairs to put my arms around Harold. The smell of his hair enters my nostrils and makes the circuit: lungs, bloodstream, heart.

～

Patsy works, full-time and intent. She's in charge of the St. Boniface capital campaign, seeking hundreds of thousands over three years to fund major renovations. Her fingers fly over the telephone, her voice cajoles and nudges. Everyone, she says, is happy to hear from her. Finally her good deeds in the community are paying off.

She holds herself upright, standing in her office doorway. "I'm trying to keep things simple for you, Marta."

"Thank you, Patsy."

"Matthilda is at an age when she needs companionship. Summer holidays are long. Children are out of school for a good two and a half months."

"Astonishing."

She blinks at me. "Yes. So, you see, you'll have to arrange play dates with her kiddy friends. Find out who they are. Take her to their homes for a few hours. Supervise. Bring her back."

"Ah."

"That's what nannies do. They take their charges to the park. They push them on the swings. They chat with other nannies. You could pick up valuable pointers from them. What you need is a routine. It will simplify things enormously for you."

"I take Matthilda to the park."

"I don't mean the little park. Take her to Withrow Park. Pack a nutritious lunch. Stay all day."

"I'm expected to make Father Jerome's lunch at lunchtime. Besides, she doesn't want to stay all day."

"Well, make her! She can't spend the rest of her life lurking around here with you!"

I've hardly even started bonding with Matthilda, and Patsy is scheming to pull us apart.

∾

"How old are you, Marta?" Matthilda asks. There is no television set at the rectory. We have made one out of a box, but now that it's finished we don't want to watch it.

Asha would have turned six yesterday. "I'm almost twenty-seven," I say. "Twenty-six and ten-twelfths."

"You're twelves?"

"Yes. Twelfths. My birthday is in two months."

"My birthday is in September."

"Mine, too," I say. "September tenth."

"I think that's pretty old," Matthilda says. "Mine is September four. I'm going to be five."

I say nothing. The television says nothing. Matthilda is staring at it.

"When you're a hundred, I'm going to be . . ." Her voice trails off.

("Mommy, when you're a hundred, how old will I—")

"Seventy-eight."

"Will you still be alive then?"

"When you're seventy-eight?" I shrug. "You'll be a mommy then. Maybe even a grandma. Do you think I'll be alive then?"

"Yup. 'Cause you'll be a great-grandma then, right?"

I give her a squeeze. "Your mom will be a great-grandma."

"But your . . . Oh, yeah. Don't worry. My mom can share."

She thinks for a moment, then says, "I know how to make a garden."

"You do?"

"Yup. You do, too."

"How do you know?"

She points at the box. "The TV. It had a gardening show."

"I didn't realize the TV was on."

"The sound was off. But that's okay. All we got to do is plant things."

"There's no room for a garden here, Matthilda. We can't mess up the parking spots out back."

"But in the front."

"There are tulips there already."

"Only leaves. They're not nice. We need something with flowers."

"Like what?"

"Something that starts with *M*."

"Marigolds?"

"Matthilda Marta marigolds?"

"I think they have them on the Danforth."

She sprawls forward and switches off the cardboard television.

There is a proper long-handled spade in the basement—excuse enough to buy a compact shrub from Sun Valley's garden centre. I'm sweating with exertion as I carry it back to the rectory. The pot grows warm and weighty in my arms.

Matthilda uses a plastic sand shovel to open holes in the dry soil near the porch. She pats in unnaturally golden flowers and uses the pads of her fingers to press crumbling earth around them.

My heart speeds as I dig. The soil is hard and clumped, stiff. I ram in the spade and haul it out.

Soil is a cover, a stubborn barrier. But my spade is good. My spade parts it, stabs it, pushes in, and drags out. I break through. I take ownership of the depths.

I lean on my shovel and sway to the dark red pounding behind my eyes.

∽

Dear Asha,

If I were a garden, I could hide you deep in my folds, I could press you close to my core. Carry you through the seasons, my roots growing around your limbs. I could keep you in the cradle of my coolness, keep you for years untold.

Bust into bloom and wither, sleep, wilt and drink and grow for you . . .

∽

Matthilda bends over her marigolds, waiting for insects to land on the flowers.

"I'm not going to let the bugs get them like the squirrels got the tulips," she says.

With the spade as my cane, I step close to her. I lay down the tool and settle myself on the patchy grass at the edge of the small strip of garden.

The sun gleams on the top of Matthilda's head. I slip an arm around her waist and pull her against me. "I don't think you have to worry about flies or ants."

"What eats them, then?"

"I'm not sure. Maybe beetles."

"With shiny backs? That kind?"

"Probably nothing will eat them. You see marigolds all the time; they seem to last."

"I'll just watch them"—she pushes away from me and goes

back to squatting—"just in case. They might need protection. There might be beetles."

A car drives by, one of Mrs. Oland's friends. I wrap my arms around my knees.

"A lady I know used to sit in her garden for hours," I say. "Not watching her flowers, just sitting."

"Is she gone, too?" Matthilda must think everyone I know has vanished.

"No, but she's very old. You might've noticed her in church, the very old lady who sits way at the front."

She picks up a twig and scratches the soil around the flower. "I wish some bugs would come."

"Bugs have to eat, too."

"Why do they have to eat *my* flowers?" She pokes between the petals with her stick.

Cars flash by as I watch Matthilda work. Her face is intense with concentration. Somewhere there may be danger; something might hide a bug.

I reach out and stroke her hair away from her face. "Would you like to have lunch beside our garden?" I ask. "We can keep an eye on your flowers."

When the sun goes down, I climb into bed knowing the rolling credits of failure will begin.

I could see that I should . . .

My father would hear us tonight . . .

I know them well. One is my fault, two is my folly, every number a mistake, every line a strike against me.

Tonight I strike back.

"*Matthilda*," I say.

If I push hard enough . . .

"*Matthilda*," I say.

I disrupt the script again and again. Yes, there is failure. But there is also progress.

Do you hear me? *Matthilda*.

30

MORNING: FACE THE DAY. I'm up and getting dressed when Matthilda enters my room. I didn't expect to see her today, a Saturday. I didn't hear her. How silently she can move.

My room, with its small draped window, is eternally in half-darkness. Even the dangling ceiling lamp can barely brighten the surrounding greyness.

Matthilda passes easily through the duskiness, slipping around me and climbing into my bed. Her body tucks into the warm tangle of cotton I've recently shoved aside.

"Sleep tight, Matthilda," I say quietly.

She closes her eyes. Even in this darkness I can see her smile.

I want to ask Father Jerome about temptation. Does he struggle against it? Does he triumph?

And then what? What of the thoughts he has subdued, the images wrestled aside? Does he cast them away and pray to forget them?

Does he first let them linger, and let himself wish they could be real—as I do with my memories and my invisible letters to Asha?

I don't ask; I make his breakfast. He presided over a special Mass this morning, and he never eats beforehand. Patsy sits conversing with him while Matthilda snuggles alone in my bed. He sprinkles All-Bran into a bowl of Cheerios. I mix a batch of pancakes, and Patsy chooses her words carefully.

"The problem is not with future funds. The pledges have been phenomenal—tens of thousands, from families and even individuals, to come in over the next three years. I've even been promised a few bequeathals."

"Sounds great."

"Yes. It sounds great."

"But?"

"Harcourt and Moore expect a significant instalment before they'll so much as put up the hoarding. We don't have an instalment. We have nothing in hand. We have promises."

"No cheques?"

"Piddling, stingy amounts. Twenty dollars from a family of five. Mr. Maxwell gave fifty. I probably spent that much bringing him soup last fall when his son disappeared. I've made four phone calls to Anita Nesbitt."

"And?"

"And I've got nothing yet."

"Nothing? She's always been a great supporter."

"She's pledged five hundred over two years. I would've thought, for someone in her position . . ."

"We're not the only ones asking for their money, Patsy. People have a lot of financial commitments these days."

"Well, I have a lot of commitments, too. I have a child and a husband. I have a house to look after. But that doesn't stop me from dropping everything in order to deal with Ms. Nesbitt's ethical dilemmas or Mr. Maxwell's despair. This parish wouldn't be the same if some of us didn't keep on giving all the time."

"And we appreciate your—"

"The Carson boy who overdosed a few years ago. Do you remember that? Matthilda was barely walking and she had one thing after another: colds, chicken pox, impetigo, roseola. Do you know how much time I spent with my own daughter that winter? I was at the Carson house every Sunday after church. Drilling sense into the boy. Keeping the family together. Who else would have done that for them? Who in this parish lifts a single finger to help another?"

"You're a great model for us."

"Does anyone remember what someone does for them? Does anyone think about that when I call them and ask for just a tiny bit back? Even a hundred dollars right now would be enough to get us going. A hundred dollars from each family, and we would be up and running."

Father Jerome smiles at me as I place a stack of pancakes before him. He digs in. "Persevere, Patsy. You're doing a good job."

She pushes back her chair and heads toward the office.

"Who are the Carsons?" I ask.

"I don't think you'd know them," Father Jerome replies. "They haven't come to Mass in years."

"Not at St. Boniface."

He nods, reaching for the syrup bottle. "Not at St. Boniface."

∞

When Father Jerome goes out after breakfast, I trudge upstairs to straighten his room. He tells me not to clean on weekends, but what else is there to do?

I find a sock under his blankets and a Kleenex under his pillow. Without thinking, I throw the sock in the wastebasket and toss the tissue toward the laundry basket. It drifts to the floor.

I'm scooping the sock out of the bedside wastebasket when something in there catches my eye.

"Marta?" Patsy's voice drifts up the stairs. "I'm just running out for a while. Matthilda's staying. Keep an eye on her, if you would. She's in my office, drawing. She hasn't had lunch yet; fix her something soon."

"Right," I call back distractedly. I sit on the bed with the wastebasket in my lap and my hand poised over its contents.

There's a Polaroid in there, cut into pieces.

I reach in gingerly. I sift through notes and junk mail, napkins from Pizza Pizza, a leaky pen, an empty, clear plastic identification badge, crumpled receipts, a *Toronto Life* magazine. I pull out glossy slices of the photograph and put the puzzle together on the bed. The image grows in shards and suggestions.

I am as confused as ever.

The background shows Father Jerome's dresser with one open drawer. In front of it, in the photograph's centre, the emulsion has been pressed and manipulated into a mishmash of colours. The person who stood or knelt there is gone, has become gibberish.

Perhaps it was not a person at all. It could have been a stool or a chair, a floor lamp, or a pair of boots. Perhaps the scrawl of emulsion is not large enough to enclose a person. Unless it were a small person. Unless it were a child.

Whatever it was, the subject is now unrecognizable. Its image has been obliterated.

Or this was once just a picture of a dresser, and now the pressure on the photo is the subject in itself.

Patsy appears at the bedroom door. I drop the discarded magazine over the jagged mosaic on the bed.

"Will you answer me?" she demands. "I said I can't find my umbrella. I'm going to the McCabes'. Where did you put my umbrella?"

Patsy's project list is ever growing: Mr. McCabe, whose faith was shaken when a streetcar broke his hip; Laura Miller, who is agitating to remove the Scout troop from the church basement; the young man from Tim Hortons doughnut shop whose girlfriend is considering an abortion.

"You took it home on Thursday," I say.

She blinks at me. She smiles sweetly, showing her teeth. "I knew you'd know where it is! Well, see you soon. I'll be back in no time. Matthilda won't be any trouble, I'm sure. She's happy as a clam."

I smile my most saccharine smile. Matthilda is no trouble, never any trouble at all.

I finish tidying Father Jerome's room and decide not to empty his wastebasket today. I can't take the Polaroid pieces with me. Whatever else they are, they are Father Jerome's. They are as much his as is the rosary dangling from his mirror. He may yet wish to retrieve them.

I can't take them, but I hate knowing that he'll sleep beside this fractured image tonight. I sprinkle the pieces back into the wastebasket. I stir the contents, using the rolled-up magazine as a spoon. Before I leave, I grasp the doorknob. I turn it: warm, low, medium, high. I adjust it carefully. Half an hour, 350 degrees. Then I close the door and let the heat do its trick. Heat changes everything.

Already I feel the temperature rising under my fingertips. It spreads through my body as I rush down the hall. Are priests allowed to have secrets?

I descend the stairs quickly with sweat gathering along my hairline. Let this Polaroid mean nothing. Let Matthilda be colouring in the office, alone.

I reach the front hall. Matthilda glances up then returns to her work.

I exhale.

"Want a cheese sandwich," I ask, "or grilled cheese?"

She shrugs. "I don't care."

She is kneeling on the office chair with her bare, pointy elbows on Patsy's desk. She swivels her hips, in red plaid shorts, turning the chair back and forth as she draws. Her body arcs over her paper. Her calves are lean and smooth.

It's up to me.

("Pick a colour, Mommy. See? It's called a cootie catcher. I made it at school. It tells fortunes."

"Red."

"R-E-D. Pick a—"

"One."

"O-N-E. Now pick another number and I'll tell you your fortune. It's underneath the flap. Like, maybe you'll be rich, or you'll be in the newspaper or—"

"Three."

"No, Mommy, you have to pick a number that's on the flaps! There's no three.")

"Cheese," I say, "on toast. With pickles. To go."

Matthilda looks at me, puzzled.

"We'll eat on the porch. Bring your paper and crayons."

31

"I'm making you something," Matthilda says a few days later, with her elbows on my legs and her eyes sparkling up at me. I smile. She is a creative one, little Matthilda. Always drawing, cutting, gluing. Already I have filled two folders with her pictures. They are stored carefully under my cot.

"For your birthday," she says. "Something very special. But it takes a long, long time."

"You're very special," I say.

"It's not that-way special!" She frowns. "This is something I'm making!"

So many subtleties, always. "Can you tell me what it is, or is it a secret?"

"I'll whisper it, but you can't listen, okay?"

"Okay."

She puts a delicate hand to her lips and mouths the words. Then her voice tumbles into laughter and delight.

Harold has not come to the rectory today. He has not come for six days. I didn't see him in church on Sunday; neither he nor Mrs. Oland was there.

"It's not out of the ordinary," Father Jerome tells me. "Not in the least. Harold's expected only when we need him. Of course, sometimes he drops in just to visit for a bit. Cup of tea, bite of lunch. But we don't have enough work to bring him in every day. Or even every week, for that matter."

I know that. That's not the point.

"To tell the truth," he says, "we probably don't have enough work here to justify bringing him in at all. Patsy did the figures, and for the same cost, we could—"

"But Harold needs to come here."

Father Jerome nods. "Of course he does. Yes, indeed! And we're glad to have him. It's just that his sort of fixing is self-perpetuating, if you know what I mean." He smiles.

Self-perpetuating. Patsy would never use such a sophisticated word with me.

"When a pull chain falls off a light, he ties a string on." Father Jerome chuckles. Each *"heh heh"* jostles his slender body like a tic. "When the string snaps, he ties a shoelace to the stub of the string. The more Harold helps us, the worse the rectory looks." Father Jerome looks happy.

"Then why do you keep asking him back?"

He is silent for a moment, smiling serenely. "You just told me yourself, Marta. Harold needs to come here."

I wish Harold would come back.

I pull a chair away from Father Jerome's desk. He nods, and I sit down.

"I had a child once, Father," I begin.

"Yes, I know."

I wonder what I want to say. I go on anyway.

"My father never met her."

Father Jerome raises an eyebrow. He leans back in his chair. "Is your father living?"

"He's alive. I stopped seeing him when I was expecting."

"And so . . ."

"So that was that."

Father Jerome casts his eyes down. I look at his hands on the edge of the desk. They are small. When he speaks again, his voice is unevenly modulated, as it is during his sermons.

"The past is past, Marta. No, we don't always do the best thing. No, your father will not have a chance to meet your daughter now. Do the reasons really matter?"

"Of course they matter."

"Does your father even know you had a child?"

I can't believe how the question hits me. It opens up chasms of astonishment. My father knows nothing.

How could I have denied him the knowledge?

I had not wanted the man who avoided my gaze in his kitchen, while I avoided him altogether, to be connected to my child. I had feared the possibility. Surely I could not have kept my distance from my mother and kept my ties with my father.

I had not thought my omission would be more than temporary. Just until I was settled, and strong, and secure . . .

Did I really not tell him of Kurt's rages? Of my despair or my pregnant hopes? Of Asha's birth? Of fire?

Did I never speak to him of loss?

Did I spare him all this?

Is it possible that I loved him that much?

∽

I hear the front door open. Patsy appears in the doorway and I get up to leave Father Jerome's office. She lets me pass, then calls after me.

"Where's Matthilda?"

"Upstairs, doing crafts. I'll tell her you're back."

"I've just popped in to pick up some papers. I have to scoot out again in a minute." Patsy glances into the office then comes over to me. Her voice drops. "Marta," she says, "I want to talk to you about that, the craft thing. Do you think it's okay?"

"What?"

"You know. Matthilda always doing crafts, nothing but crafts."

I shrug. "Sure. What's the harm in it?"

"Doesn't it seem rather obsessive to you? She's only four. She should have a wider range of interests."

"Four-year-olds can't have interests without making them obsessions. They take to plush animals and their bedrooms become zoos. If they like some TV character, it's got to be on their sheets, their pyjamas, their T-shirts, their—"

"That is a matter of upbringing. I'm not talking about greed. I'm very careful about managing Matthilda's possessions."

"I didn't say it was greed. It's passion. It's not enough to like horses; four-year-olds live to own one. If Matthilda knew how to sew, I guarantee you she'd be living with a needle in her hand, making little stuffed pillows and her own Halloween costume. And she could do it, too. She's so good with her hands. She learns very quickly and—"

"For heaven's sake. The last thing I want is for Matthilda to sew! Are you not hearing me? This craft obsession is out of control. I don't know what to do with all the things she makes! It's ridiculous. Can't you steer her toward something more active?"

"If she wants to be active, I won't stop her. I'll take her swimming or whatever, if you want. But don't expect me to tell her she can't make things. I'm not going to make her miserable."

Patsy's mouth is a straight line. She glares at me but her voice is sweet. "I'll bet you sew, don't you, Marta?"

(*"I don't want to do this, Mama! I want to sew."*

"This is sewing."

"No. It isn't. I want to use the machine."

"First, you pin. Then you baste the pieces together by hand with a running stitch. And then you sew it all on the machine."

"But you don't do that. You don't baste. You just pin a bit and sew."

"This is how you learn. If you do it right and carefully the first time, you don't have to do it all over again."

"I don't need to learn. I just want to sew!"

"Oh, Marta! Fine. Go to the machine. Go. Teach yourself if that's the way you want it.")

Patsy's voice is light and curious, but there is suspicion in it. "You probably learned to sew at Matthilda's age. Am I right? I do have a sense for people."

"I know how to sew," I say.

(*"Oh damn! The lady's coming in an hour and I still have to—"*

"It's okay. I'll hem the skirt while you finish the collar. Okay, Mama?"

"Just make sure you—"

"I can do it! Or I'll do the collar and you—"

"You can't do this part, Marta. You hem."
"I'm hemming."
"Later I'll teach you about collars.")

I put my hand on Patsy's shoulder and look solemnly into her eyes. "I promise not to teach it to your daughter."

∞

It turns out that sewing is the last thing on Matthilda's mind.

"Can we go out today, Marta? I'm bored of always the same things. My mom won't care. When she gets back from her meeting, she'll have tons of work to do."

"I know, sweetie. And I'm sure your mom would love it if we went out today. But she wants me to wash the floor after lunch. Later this afternoon we'll go out. Why don't you bring down your craft stuff? We'll have lunch, then I'll get the mopping done, then we'll go to the park."

"It's always crafts. You think all I like is crafts."

"Well, what do you like then, Matthilda?"

"Nothing. And I don't want to go out either."

I crouch down to look into her face.

"Okay," I say. "Get your sun hat."

∞

I push Matthilda on the swing. Back and forth. Forward and back.

"Push me higher, Marta! To the sky!"

("Frankly, ma'am, those old cars blow up easily. Just like in the movies.")

∞

When we return, Matthilda climbs the stairs on her hands and feet, then lies flat on the shaded front porch.

"Up," I say.

"In a minute. It's nice. Come feel."

I slip the key into the lock and nudge the door open.

Patsy's voice comes from Father Jerome's office, close and clear. "—too much time together! Always upstairs with puzzle pieces and construction paper everywhere, or holed up in that dank back room she sleeps in. They spend whole days at the kitchen table. It's not healthy how they stick to each other."

"Matthilda seems quite happy."

"Marta spoils her rotten! She's lost all her independence. She whines at home now, she wants things—"

"She whines? I thought she was seeming very content these days."

"With all due respect, Father, you've never had children. They show you one face but it's something else inside. The minute I walk her out of the rectory she starts sulking."

"But really, Patsy, don't all kids sulk?"

"No. Not my kid. Never whined, never sulked. Not until now. Not until Marta moved back in."

"Maybe Matthilda is just learning to let go a little, to not be so hard on herself. Maybe this is exactly what she needs now. She's only four. She doesn't have to be perfect."

"This is a long way from perfect. Mouthing back. Refusing to go out."

"Aren't they out now?"

"Oh, yes, but just watch. At the first little whine, Marta will cave in and bring her back. And she's napping her! I swear, Father, I've seen them curled up together in the middle of the afternoon. Matthilda hasn't needed a nap for two years! It's Marta that's needy. There's something not right about how she's attached herself to Matthilda. She's turning her away from me."

"Patsy, it's your decision. But give yourself time to think about it. It seems to me that Matthilda has really blossomed lately. And I believe Marta is truly fond of her."

"Fine. I'll think. But if you want me to keep working on the campaign then you think of something too, Father. I want my daughter back."

32

I CANNOT DUST TODAY. I know what dust is made of, old skin spun plush. Today I can't muster the courage to muck around with it.

Matthilda has been cranky all morning, and though it is barely lunchtime, my patience and energy are wearing thin. She didn't give me a smile when Patsy handed her over before leaving for a string of appointments.

Her jump rope, with stuffed animals tied to each end, sprawls through the front hall. I've told her twice to move it. Now Father Jerome stumbles over it as he approaches with an envelope in his hand, and Matthilda huffs her protest.

There is news. It came in a card this morning. The envelope is addressed to Father Jerome, but the card inside says, *"To Marta: Perhaps you should know that my mother is not well. She is expected to leave us at any moment. As of this writing she is in Room 279 at St. Agatha's Comprehensive Care Unit on Monterey Road West. Yolanda Oland-Edgar."*

Of course I go. I put together a quick lunch, toss a juice box, a bottle of sunscreen, and some books in a bag, and salvage a folding stroller from the lost-and-found under the basement stairs. The stroller will be small for Matthilda, but her eyes are red and heavy, and I am hoping she'll nap.

On the bus I consider what I may find. Perhaps Mrs. Oland will greet me feebly, holding out skeletal hands. Perhaps she is not so ill after all. She may wish for my help with a few remaining possessions. She may even have a small box marked "Marta Fett." But surely it will not be so. I am no one's beloved, I have no way to help, I may already be too late.

Matthilda whines as the stifling hot bus plods along, as she sways in my lap in our seat. When I squeeze her into the stroller on the sidewalk in front of the hospital, she immediately settles in with drooping eyelids and slack lips. In the lobby I request directions in a whisper. A hospital volunteer leans across her desk to peer at Matthilda, then holds up fingers and mouths numbers: *Two seven nine.* She points to an elevator.

We go up to Mrs. Oland's room, and I push open the door. Calling quietly, with my hands tight on the stroller handles, I step inside.

The room is not small. The paint, when I look at it, is a soothing blue. When I don't look directly at it, it is dull grey.

Matthilda is sleeping, slumped, her hands fallen open with the palms turned up. When I kneel to straighten her, gently easing her toward the sloping back of the stroller seat, she rolls forward again, her body seeking the familiar.

I am loath to bring her with me into this parting.

I smooth down the muss of hair on her damp head. I leave the stroller near the wall and step away. Finally I allow myself to scan the room.

There is much emptiness between where I stand and the middle bed of three, the only one occupied. I have heard this quiet before: a voiceless crystal pitch.

I enter it.

Mrs. Oland sleeps, breath uncommitted, barely passing the pale mauve lips and silvery teeth. Soft, clear tubing lies horizontal across her face; two small blunt horns direct oxygen to her nostrils.

She is older now than ever before. Of course: We all are. But Mrs. Oland has aged to the edge of death. There is no sentimentality in me; it would be clear to anyone. She lies hesitating at the end of her life as if waiting for final directions.

Beside her bed there is a small storage unit. A glass vase with three carnations sits on top. There is a crusty ring an inch above the waterline; the water has evaporated to below some of the stems.

I pull up a chair and look closely at Mrs. Oland's face.

I think about her parcels. Were they sent by Lawrence Edgar? Did the beloveds receive the gifts, the innuendoes, the carefully chosen inheritances? Did they phone with their thanks, their anger, and their curiosity? It seems wrong that I do not know the answers. After all of Mrs. Oland's shared intentions and whispered confidences, her sly, proud smiles, she alone knows the results of her naïve manipulations.

Were there phone calls, cards, silence? I imagine her waiting for the telephone to ring, for the mail to arrive. Waiting to measure her success, to confirm the potency of her influence. Unable to stop herself from hoping and waiting.

How long it must have seemed.

I imagine the responses that may have come, the beloveds who conveyed their thanks with relief or impatience.

"So you've finally taken the plunge. That's a load off your mind, I suppose."

"I don't know what you were thinking, but it's the thought that counts."

"Are you sure you've sent out everything? Maybe you should ask that Marta girl."

I want to believe that Mrs. Oland did not hear those voices, nor the silence of those too arrogant to call.

She should have kept the parcels at home until the end. I should have stayed with her to ensure it. She should have let herself go, gone first, before loosening her grip on her things.

I know she did not. I know what has brought her here, to this hospital bed, already. Not cancer, not age—for why not live to ninety?—but disappointment and despair. She made a mistake. She relinquished control. She lost everything: her possessions, her hope, her mission. Now she lies here, expected to give up more.

How can she?

And how can she not?

"Just go," I whisper.

Her eyelids are still and almost without lashes. Her cheek-bones shine through her skin. The oxygen flows into her body through her thin nose. I repress the urge to pull the tube away. I sit watching the weak breath move her chest.

Will you go forward now, Mrs. Oland? Alone again, finally alone?

The question grows. The minutes pass.

Then I realize that my head has been dropping lower and lower. My face is scant inches from Mrs. Oland's parted lips.

She breathes in my breath. I cannot take it away.

In the hallway the rubber soles of a nurse's shoes pad by. The cloying perfume of hyacinth drifts in.

My hair hangs close to Mrs. Oland's. It brushes against her thin strands, curls against the tube across her cheeks. My fore-head feels the pull of the pillow, its sterile, anonymous comfort.

My eyes are tired. Lids heavy.

(*"Hear the waves . . ."*)

∽

Dear Asha,

You had a grandfather. Do you know that? Of course you know. You know everything now.

Is there nothing more I can tell you?

∽

I should whisper to Mrs. Oland of beaches, of sand. Your favourite book, Mrs. Oland, on your frail, narrow chest . . .

I could go with her. I could place my mouth on hers, let her drain the air from my lungs. Clasp her to me and sink into nothingness together, as close as a mother and child.

My heart pounds with sudden yearning and envy. With an effort, I bring my hand to the oxygen tube that crosses her face. I would release her to death, if only she would do the same for me. If only she could.

The skin of Mrs. Oland's face is loose and finely lined, as yielding as whipped cream. My hand sinks into her cheek. The walls of teeth press against my palm.

Then a faint sound rises, gently disturbing the moment. A slight and trembling breath. The sigh of a dreaming child.

I lift my eyes and see a drop of clear, sweet saliva form on Matthilda's lip. In a moment it will fall.

I turn away from the bed. I do not say goodbye.

I do not wait for Mrs. Oland to leave.

33

MATTHILDA IS MAKING SOMETHING with Father Jerome. He is teaching her. She tells me so. She looks unhappy.

"Aren't you enjoying it?" I ask.

She shakes her head.

"Can you tell me what it is?"

She looks at the kitchen floor. The linoleum is beige and brown, patterned with irregular circular shapes pushed against each other. It's easy to see faces in it. Angry faces. Men's faces. All the women I see in it are old. Old and disappointed. Matthilda crouches down and traces the pictures she finds in the lines. She sees leopards, cats, dinosaurs.

"Matthilda? What is Father Jerome teaching you?"

"He told me not to tell."

My lips are dry. I lift the kettle and fill it. I put it on the burner, then sit beside the kitchen table which flares with too-bright sunshine.

"Come here," I say. "Come on."

Matthilda gets up.

I pull her onto my lap and lean my head against hers. "You told me before that you were making me something. Remember? A secret something."

"I know that. I am. I told you I am. But I never told you *what*."

"I didn't say you did. But that was a while ago. You've been working on it for a long time. Don't you want to make it any more?"

"It's too hard."

"Then don't do it."

Matthilda doesn't reply.

"Can't you make something else instead?"

"No! My mom says you have to finish whatever you start."

"What does Father Jerome say?"

Matthilda fidgets. She jerks her head away then brings it back quickly, and it smacks into my ear. I hold her a little tighter.

"Did Father Jerome say you should finish it?"

She starts swinging her feet. Her heels batter my shins. "He said not to say anything. He said it was our secret."

"Secrets shouldn't always be secrets, Matthilda."

She looks at me suspiciously.

"Sometimes it's better to tell. Sometimes it helps fix problems."

"That's not true. Father Jerome said I can't tell. He said when we close the door of his room it's like a reminder for us to keep our lips zipped shut. And then we open the door after, and that reminds us to keep our eyes and ears open against temptation."

"Against temptation? What does he mean, temptation?"

"You know. Like now. How you're trying to make me say."

Temptation. I take a deep breath and steady my voice. "Does he ever take your picture when he's teaching you?"

She glares at me. Her eyes are almost sparking with anger, but there is something else there, too. Either recognition or curiosity. I move quickly to take advantage of it. "What is he teaching you, Matthilda?"

She knows I am setting her up. Her lip trembles. "You just want me to get in trouble," she says. She slips off my lap and stomps out.

("There's something I need to tell you, Asha. A secret."
"Another secret? Daddy told me one, too."
"He did? Daddy told you a secret?"
"Yup."
"What was it?"
"That's a secret!"
"Asha . . ."
"Ha! Is that funny? My secret is a secret. That's funny!"
"Please, listen. Asha, come here."
"It's a secret, Mommy. I'm not telling.")

It is so quiet here today. I sit in the kitchen, coffee in hand, worrying, getting up, sitting down. Wishing Harold were here. There are no leaking taps, no broken doorknobs, no minor repairs pending. It's lonely when the place isn't falling apart.

Patsy is out campaigning for dollars, and Matthilda is upstairs with Father Jerome again. Every few minutes I lean into the hallway to listen to their murmurs. I creep up a few stairs, compelled by their silence. I return to my seat at the table. I am on my third mug of coffee; the first two turned stone cold.

It is a hot summer day, and Father Jerome is teaching

Matthilda to make something. They are in his room, a room I enter daily. I have closed the door behind me and tried to read the energy there. I have looked in drawers and in the waste-basket. I have scanned his objects, but they are few and mean-ingless: respectable books, rosaries, his weights languishing in the closet, his dresser decorated with thank-you cards. I have peered into his mirror as though I could find his face there. I have checked the pockets of cardigans in his closet. What can you find in a pocket? What can you find anywhere? There is no evidence of teaching in that room. There is no evidence of anything.

There is only Father Jerome and Matthilda, and their secret something, and me in the kitchen listening to nothing.

A lifetime ago, I sat like this in my own small kitchen, drinking strong black coffee, while three blocks away Asha sat at her school desk learning about moths and butterflies.

(*"Butterflies have six legs. Moths have furry antennae. Mommy, I told you that was a moth I saw."*)

A billion blades of grass ago, a thousand sheets of news-paper, a hundred buckets of water.

Today the coffee is milder. The acid has been tempered. Everything that could happen to me has happened.

Why don't I learn? The child upstairs is not mine.

I'm washing out my coffee cup when Harold strides into the kitchen. I turn, relieved. There are almost tears in my eyes. There is mischief in his smile.

"I got nothing to do today, Marta!" he says. "I woke up this morning and said I got another day off. But before I knew it I was on my way here anyways. I guess I just can't stay away that long!"

I laugh. "That's the problem with you workaholics. You don't know how to relax. Sit down. Stick around. I'm sure Father Jerome will find something for you to fix."

"I was thinking we could take a break. You could take a break, and then we could go out and we could get a coffee at a doughnut shop. Or if you want, we could go to the library or something. Or I guess if you have any shopping to do . . ."

The kitchen seems so sunny with Harold in it. I almost take his hand. I almost pull him into a chair.

"I can't go out now, Harold. I'm watching Matthilda. Patsy's in and out all day. But I'll make some fresh coffee. Hold on. It'll just take a minute."

Harold sits down, slightly awkward but still smiling, and looks around while I measure grounds and water. I flick on the coffee machine and sit across the table from him.

"Where have you been?" I ask quietly.

He glances away from me. His fingertips with their dirty nails start tapping the table in unison, all of them but his thumbs.

"Just gone," he says. "Can't be gone and be here. That's the problem."

"Is everything okay?"

His fingers splay on the tabletop. "I'm not on the payroll. I don't have to be here every day like you."

"But sometimes you—"

"Sometimes I can be here, sometimes I can't. I got other things I have to do sometimes."

"Like what?"

"Like—" He stops. The kitchen is quiet. Then Harold's gaze shifts to his hands. He turns them so the palms face up. "Like not be here."

I think about that. "Sometimes," I say.

"Yeah."

"Be anywhere but here."

"Just be out, outside. Just not be here."

"Okay."

I look at him until he raises his head and meets my eyes. Then I keep looking at him until he lets my smile sink in and he begins, cautiously, to smile back.

I get up and pour our coffees, black for me, double-double for Harold.

"Contractor coffee," I say, putting his cup down. He taught me the term and the meaning, too: double cream, double sugar. (*"How they drink it in the trades. You might start off different, but soon you're drinking contractor coffee like the other guys."*)

I settle into my chair. "You worked with a team once, didn't you, Harold? A construction team . . . or renovations . . ."

He laughs. "It's crew, Marta. Not team." He keeps chuckling as he raises his cup to his lips.

I smile and don't press the question. Harold is always happy when he is teaching me something. He has shown me how to join electrical wires by twisting them together and screwing a little plastic cap onto them—though he forgot what the cap was called. He has explained to me about halogen light bulbs, how touching them with your fingertips will make them burn out or explode. I let him tell me about painting walls, the importance of cutting in the corners and edges with a brush first, even though I knew it all and had seen it done much better many times.

With Harold happy, the kitchen has a comfortable glow; I feel it enveloping me. Now that Harold is here, won't

Matthilda want to come into the kitchen, too? Surely it would be okay, it would be right, to bring her out of Father Jerome's room now.

I push back my chair. "I should go find Matthilda. She'll be so glad you're back."

I say it, but don't move.

"Want me to fetch her?" Harold asks. His hands spread flat on the table.

"No," I say.

Harold waits.

I say, "You know Father Jerome."

He grins. "That's a funny question."

"I mean, you've known him for a long time."

"Uh-huh. Way long. I known him since we were kids."

"Kids! I didn't know that."

"He lived in our house. Him and his family. My dad was the landlord. That's how Jerome knew I knew how to fix things and stuff. It was an old house." He smiles again. "Something always needed fixing."

"So you and Father Jerome have kept in touch all this time?"

"No. I didn't see him for years. Then I came to the church and there he was. Up front. Saying the sermon and all. He was a priest. So I kept coming back and he didn't kick me out. And then, after a while, he gave me things to do here. That was the start of my job."

"What do you mean, he didn't kick you out?"

"You know. I didn't have a place to live then. I was a home-less person."

I sigh.

Harold had a father and a mother and a sister. Father Jerome had the same. Two equal families lived in the same house on Nickel Street. One up, one down. One as owners, one as tenants. Now Harold the handyman sleeps in a temporary shelter for men and upholds the semblance of a trade at the rectory, while Father Jerome writes sermons and dabbles in weight-lifting.

"We weren't friends," Harold tells me. "He didn't really have friends. He was so smart. Super smart. Mostly he stayed home and read books. I garbage-picked an old typewriter for him. He put it in the sunroom at the front. After dinner you could see him in there typing, sometimes with a blanket around his shoulders. I was out playing, running around. I kind of collected everything. I was always out looking. I was always seeing him all lit up in the front room there. I couldn't see his hands. But I could hear them."

Father Jerome was writing. Perhaps he is teaching Matthilda to write.

"His sister was called Carol. She hated everybody. That was kind of funny. She was like a cat, you know? Hissy."

"She was younger?"

"Yeah. For a while she liked my sister Enid. Then Carol went back to her old friends, but by then Enid was kind of hissy, too. My mom loved Carol, though. She thought she was the funniest little thing."

I purse my lips. "How did Fa— How did Jerome feel about Carol?"

Harold shrugs. "You know Father Jerome. He thinks the same about everyone, I guess. I could never really get his ideas. He's smart but, you know, he's sort of different."

∞

Harold follows me up the stairs and down the narrow hallway, past the bathroom, past Father Jerome's closed bedroom door. I lead him to the unoccupied room at the front of the house, where Matthilda's baskets of plush toys and craft supplies overflow.

"You know what?" I say lightly. "I think Matthilda's in with Father Jerome. In his room."

"Oh," says Harold. He turns toward the hall. I grab the back of his shirt and he stops.

So much is missing. So much I don't know.

I say, "Enid."

Harold starts slightly. He crosses to the front window and sits against the ledge, eyeing me warily.

"You didn't really say anything about Enid. About her growing up. Her life."

"So?"

"So I should have asked about her. You said she got crabby."

"Hissy. Ssss." He shows his teeth.

"Well, then what?"

"What's it to you, Marta? She's my sister."

"So why don't you talk about her?"

"Because," he says, "she's my sister."

What do I know of sisters? The closest thing I had to siblings were the stories that grew with me—the death of Old Leonard, the flight of my mother.

Words catch in my throat. I don't know how to say what I should say.

Harold hefts himself off the window ledge. He takes two slow steps toward me and lays his fingertips on my T-shirt, below the hollow of my throat. He lets his fingers rest there.

They calm me.

"I'm just being silly," I say. I give him a small smile.

He smiles back. "I'm famous for that. For being silly. But it can get to you. Don't you get tired of people not taking you serious?"

"You're not silly."

"Yeah, I know. Neither are you. So. What's up?"

My smile stiffens. "Just that Father Jerome is teaching Matthilda something." How many times have I told myself that? It means only what it means.

He drops his hand. "Yeah. I know that."

"You do? Well, what is he teaching her, then?"

Harold looks irritated. "I don't know. But something. She was in there with him when I went to check the phone jack. That was a few weeks ago, I guess."

"A few weeks ago! Where was I?"

"Maybe doing laundry? I don't know, Marta! It's not like you gotta keep your eyes on Matthilda every minute. She never had that before you came here, you know."

I am startled by the bite of hostility behind his words. This isn't the gentle angel Harold I am used to. I have violated something with my questions, with my concerns.

From my angle to the window, I see no rooftops nor chimneys, only treetops. A squirrel scurries up a branch and leaps to another, limbs stretching, skin webbing, to land dangling by its front paws. A cicada begins its sharply mournful drone. Are there people out there? Does it all continue while we gather in this upstairs room, playing with words and doing nothing?

(*"Mommy, who's more important, me or God?"*)

I spin to face Harold. He is leaning against the door frame.

"Why?" I ask. "Why does Father Jerome want to spend all that time with her? Doesn't that seem a little strange to you?"

Harold's shoulder twitches. His voice is tight and controlled. "You tell me, Marta."

"Maybe something is going on."

His breath catches.

I walk over to him. It is time for care, for quiet. I put a hand on his chest, hoping to ease his heart as he did mine. His blood is a drumfire under my fingertips.

He doesn't say anything; he looks at my hand.

I whisper through a crack in my throat. "I just want her to be safe. You know; you understand. I'm not accusing Father Jerome, but . . ."

His head snaps up. His teeth are gritted. "Not accusing him of what?"

I step back; my hand drops. "Why are they in there? What are they doing?"

"They're making something."

"I know. A surprise." I speak in a fast, sour whisper. "They're making something for me and I should just butt out."

"You can't go accusing people."

I sneer. "I should wait and see. Until something happens." The words taste ugly in my mouth.

"Stop it, Marta!" Harold lurches. He grabs my upper arms. "You don't know nothing about what's happening. You can't know."

"You're always saying that. 'You can't know.' I should stand here and not do anything because I can't know for sure. Because I don't know what they're doing in the room right next door."

"They're making something for you!"

"Open your eyes, Harold! You think he can't do wrong because of what he is?"

"He's a good man."

"I'm a good woman, and I let my own daughter be killed!"

Harold's grip collapses. His fingers slide slowly down my arms until they curl like bangles around my wrists.

My hands are cold. I ball them into fists and tuck them into the curve of Harold's palms.

Harold's eyes are rimmed in pink. He closes his hands on mine, holds them still.

But he cannot still the trembling of my voice. "It's true, Harold. I could have saved her. But I didn't. I didn't do anything. My husband drove off with her, and she never came back."

"That isn't your fault."

"She could have been here with me. You could have been throwing her like a sack of potatoes and making her laugh like Matthilda."

"She was shy, too?"

"I don't know. I don't know how she was with people. I only know with me."

"Then, with you?"

"She was . . . I don't know. She was like a part of me. I was hardly without her. I hardly let her out of my sight."

(*"Can I go to Lucy's after school? Please?"*

"Not today, Asha."

"Tomorrow?"

"I don't think so."

"Another day?"

"Ask me then."

"You always say that.")

". . . until the very end. I was planning to take her and leave my husband."

"You were getting ready?"

"I was putting it off. I left her with Kurt while I went shopping. I was getting ready to fix up the house."

"And then after that, you'd leave?"

I look away. "I promised myself we would leave."

"You wouldn't lie to yourself on purpose. You just took too long."

"The car rolled and caught on fire." I stare out the window. "I finally left. Alone. Too late."

Harold's hands are strong. Workman's hands. They squeeze around mine, containing them. We stand that way, silent, until Harold speaks.

"Marta, you know, Matthilda isn't Asha."

Then a thump comes from the room next door: Matthilda's feet hitting the floor. Her voice rises. "I hate this!"

I stiffen.

"Harold," I say, "this isn't good." But he is gripping my hands in his.

Matthilda's voice, teary: "That's not true! It's awful!"

Harold squeezes harder. "It's normal," he says.

"Let go of me, Harold."

"She's just frustrated," he says. "She's fine," but his eyes flit toward the door.

We hear Father Jerome now, his insistent tone, but the words are indistinguishable.

In my mind's eye I see him reach for her. My whole body bristles.

Then we hear her: "Get off me!"

I yank my hands out of Harold's. At the same time, Matthilda cries, "Let go!"

Harold and I bolt.

I get there first. I throw myself against the door and land in the room.

Their eyes widen. Matthilda, standing inches from the door with her mouth petulant, holds a half-finished red scarf in the air, the knitting needles crossed like swords. Father Jerome is leaning down from his perch on the edge of the bed, his own wool a pile of yellow in his lap. He is reaching toward the floor for Matthilda's rolling ball of wool. Between the ball and the scarf, red yarn drapes crazily from Matthilda's arms, snags on the buttons of her shirt, and spirals around her calves. It flattens under her feet and catches on a nailhead in the floor.

It takes an instant to capture the scene, even less time to know that all is well.

But before my shoulders can ease down, before I breathe, Harold bursts past me, knocking me against the open door. In one terrible motion, he scoops Matthilda up and veers into the hall, swiftly, his limbs agitated.

Here is what I see as I pounce after Harold: a slash of red yarn, ball spinning in pursuit of child. A knitting needle flashing to the floor.

Matthilda high, holding crimson wool over Harold's head. Harold stepping toward the stairs.

Matthilda's wool spilling like blood, puddling at Harold's feet. Harold pivoting. His foot on a tangle of wool.

Harold falling toward stairs.

Floor falling into stairwell. Harold and Matthilda falling.

Child first, small surprised face.

Harold, hands high and empty.

Shoes, soles raised.

At my feet at the top of the stairs, the slender woollen scarf lies coiled and still, as still as a serpent in sleep.

34

HAROLD IS SLOUCHED on the front steps of the rectory as I sit on this hard church pew. I feel his presence as though he were standing behind me.

Mrs. Oland's ghost sits in her customary place in the first row. I am sandwiched between two hauntings: in front, the weight of her disappointment and failure, and at my back, the heaviness of Harold's guilt.

When Mrs. Oland sent me back to live in the rectory, I let her old friends reclaim her. I stopped sitting behind her in the front left pew. I moved farther away each week, closer to the exit, away from Father Jerome's warbling sermons, his *"heh heh"* chuckles.

Now Mrs. Oland is gone and I sit at the back by habit. I have stayed, until now, on the left. But today I sit in Harold's spot to the right of the aisle.

I am compelled to represent him here. To offer myself in his place. To siphon the pity, the outrage, the judgment.

Father Jerome heard my confession yesterday.

"I let her," I began, as I always begin. "I let her die."

His voice leaped to mine: "But, Marta, she's alive!"

He turned and looked at me through the double screen. Our

eyes met in that forbidden slice of darkness, then shadows scattered across his face as he turned away.

"I'm sorry, Father," I said softly. "I meant Asha."

His voice was muffled. "Of course."

∞

Afterwards, Patsy led Harold and me into her office and sat us down. Her eyes looked as though she had been crying, but her mouth was firm.

"This type of meeting is generally known as a postmortem," she said. "Under the circumstances the term comes horribly close to home."

Harold didn't look up, and I didn't bother to explain to him what Patsy meant.

She continued. "I understand the basics of what happened. Now I'd like to hear it from everyone involved."

"Should I see if Father Jerome is finished doing confessions?" I asked.

She ignored me. "Father and Matthilda were knitting. Matthilda got upset and tangled herself up in her wool. Before Father could help her, you two burst in. Kindly take it from there."

Harold inhaled loudly, a sobbing gasp of a breath.

I said quickly, "Matthilda sounded distressed. We went to help her."

Harold's head swayed. "I'm sorry," he whispered.

"I opened the door first," I continued. "I saw that Matthilda had gotten herself into a mess and was worked up about it. But I must've been blocking Harold's view." We glanced at his bent head. "He came in behind me and picked her up."

Patsy's face was puffy. Her voice was grim. "Why did you touch her, Harold?"

He moaned.

I pulled my chair closer to Patsy's and put my hand on her forearm. "It was a mistake. My mistake. And an accident. The wool was all over the floor. I'm sure Father Jerome told you. Harold stepped on it and slipped."

Patsy looked at my hand.

I went on. "Harold would never hurt Matthilda on purpose. You know that. Neither of us would. We love Matthilda."

Patsy's chair screeched away from me. Her upper lip quivered. "You have no right," she said, "to love my daughter."

None of us is innocent. Matthilda alone lives in innocence, a small, resigned figure watching TV in a hospital bed, one arm hot and itching under its cast, one wrist wrapped with elastic bandages like an overloaded spool, her pale face quiet and composed, eyes moving in mild excitement, mild agitation, her head cradled by the padded brace encircling her neck.

I stood in her hospital room doorway yesterday after the meeting with Patsy. I stepped close and watched her breathe, watched her eyelids ripple through dreams of looking. The television played on for no one.

Matthilda slept, her bed propped up, her feet tiny peaks under a white crocheted blanket. Pink roses on the windowsill, a new purple teddy bear in the crook of her limp arm, purple fuzz clinging to the sweat of her inner elbow. The television pleaded, "Ask a parent to come into the room now, we're getting closer to our goal, we desperately need your pledge to continue the kind of programming that . . ."

I will return today, after Mass.

I sit a little higher in my pew.

The man beside me in church this morning is tall and slender—an aging professor, I think—wearing soft khakis and thick plastic-framed glasses. He hums, anticipating a psalm, a chorus, a waltz with God.

At the side of the altar, the blind cantor raises her hand, inviting the congregation to join her in song. *"Alleluia! He is risen,"* she sings. Her tight face smiles as she turns to reach for her chair.

After Asha died, after I locked my front door, after I rode the bus to Toronto and before I got on the subway, I stood in front of a pay phone and thought about my father.

What could I say to him? The quarter in my hand was a perfect circle, silver and familiar. It gave up nothing: no insight to alter my mindset, no irregularity to break my silence.

I could write on it, tiny scrawls of black marker, letters bending around the caribou's antlers and minuscule blank eyes.

Dear Papa,

I can return to you now, the way I was before. Alone. No lover, no husband, no child. I can care for you, take care of you. Except that I have no hope, Papa. I have no love. Everything has been ripped from me and there is no going forward or back.

Even my father could have no solution to that.

I would call him anyway.

I held the coin flat against the phone and shifted it toward the slot. It tipped under my fingers.

It didn't matter what he would say.

I dropped the quarter in.

It clattered down to me, down to the coin return, rejected.

I thumbed it. I pocketed it. I moved on.

The humming professor gestures with his hymn book. I've been flipping pages, delicate white waves swallowing waves.

Sunshine streams in through the high windows, warming my shoulder. I shrug it away. It flares in my periphery then fades.

Father Jerome struggles to adjust his microphone.

I cross my arms. I have my own words.

I search for words; somehow, everything needs words.

Dear Asha,

Harold is a good man. I am, perhaps, a good woman.

And yet.

There is you. There is Matthilda. Burned. Broken.

Does shame equal atonement, or pain cancel out guilt?

There is no new life here, no rebirth. Harold and I have been chosen—not to rise like the phoenix but to carry the memories we make.

No one heals us with punishment. No one rakes our cheeks or spews phlegm on our shoes.

No one lifts us out of our lives. There is nowhere to go.
No one rewrites our histories; no fear, no love, erases them.
Nothing can be purged, nothing culled or renewed.
  Fire does not make fire, only dust.

I let the last droning hymn fade away, let the intoning crowd then the last straggling parishioners pass by, before I stand up to leave the church.

As I walk toward the rectory, I see Patsy, rigid in a pale-green pantsuit, staring woodenly at Harold.

He sits on the steps, huddled into the hollows of his chest. Patsy stares, then walks away.

She has not spent much time at the rectory in the days since Matthilda's accident. She does not drop by after Mass today. She goes her way and I go mine. Mine is behind the church, in the old converted home with its two offices, its two bedrooms upstairs plus my room tucked behind the kitchen, with its dwindling cast of characters and no child for me to watch.

It is clear: I am no longer welcome at the rectory. I see it in Patsy's cloudy, distracted gaze that shifts in and out of anger. I see it in Father Jerome's weariness. It exhausts him to have me here. Who am I to add to the burden he carries? Every parishioner's sins, and my own, filter through him. What residue remains? I cannot know what clings to him, nor how heavy its weight.

Without Matthilda here, without Harold intent on repairs, we three play our roles like proverbial lost sheep. Patsy, stumbling during phone calls, falling into silences, losing focus.

Father Jerome, thoughts spiralling inward as he watches me, wondering how it came to this.

And me, a nanny without a child to watch, without a place to go.

No one knows what to do with me.

I do this: I cook, I clean. I write invisible letters, recount silent, pointless stories. I breathe into them and they shape an invisible litany.

My bag is packed and stowed under my bed with Matthilda's drawings, but where would I go? I am not leaving until Patsy or Father Jerome tells me to.

Perhaps not even then.

I recall that once in the acrid humidity of summer, I drove to a Toronto neighbourhood of hookers and art students—and fabric stores, for which I had come. I dipped into one store after another with baby Asha in my arms. I could not make myself buy even a remnant, but I soaked up the smells and fingered the textiles. Asha squirmed and nuzzled my T-shirt. My breasts swelled in warning. I vowed to leave soon, then headed to a table of taffeta.

I stopped. What was I doing, wandering through fabric stores like a drunk through bars? What was I thinking?

By the time I reached the sidewalk, Asha was wailing, wide-mouthed and frantic with hunger. Where was I to feed her? On the urine-stained corner bench, next to the man who slept there? I rushed into an ambulance station, begging for advice.

"Feed her here," the attendant said. "It's the people's ambulance service. This building belongs to you."

And so I ask now: to whom does the rectory belong?

Where should I be, and who belongs with me?

35

I HEAD TO THE HOSPITAL to see Matthilda, hoping she'll be awake this time. I am eager for reunion.

I stayed away the first few days to give her parents time alone with her after the accident. When I finally visited, yesterday, my little Matthilda was sleeping.

Even asleep, she seemed to whisper her affection for me. Her body needed sleep, but her heart knew I was there. Her fall had not broken our bond.

Perhaps Patsy will be there with Matthilda today. The possibility does not dampen my enthusiasm. Even Patsy could not cast shadows dark enough to dim the warmth Matthilda and I share. I almost hope she will be there to see it.

I hope, and she is there. Patsy, in her pale-green suit, sits on the far side of the bed. Her face reddens when she spies me.

As I approach the privacy curtain that dangles partially closed around the bed, Matthilda's pursed mouth sucks a grape from between her mother's outstretched fingers.

Before Patsy or I can speak, before I can reach Matthilda, before she realizes I am here, she wraps her hand around Patsy's and says, "Yummy Mommy," and laughs. "Can you stay with me, yummy Mommy? I like it when you're here."

Patsy smiles. "You'll like it back at home, too." She raises her chin. "Don't you miss the rectory?"

"I like here," says Matthilda. "I don't like the rectory."

I take a step back from the curtain. *She doesn't like home,* I want to hiss.

Patsy presses her point. "You like being with your mommy, isn't that right?" She proffers another grape.

Matthilda raises her purple teddy bear. "Viowet wuvs Mommy, too," she says. "Viowet wants a grape and wants Mommy to stay. Kiss Viowet, Mommy."

I feel the bile rise in my throat.

Patsy beams. "Violet is a good little bear and she has a wonderful owner. When we get home, we'll make a bed for Violet." She leans forward.

As she kisses the bear, her eyes meet mine.

Asha, what did you hear, what did you see? Did the world explode, did your eyes burst open, did Kurt reach for you?

Did he hold you, did he hold you down? Did he scream your name? Did he cry: "Sorry, Asha. Forgive me, Asha. Run."

Or: "Stay and die with me, if you love me."

Asha, take me there.

Will you not take me there?

Outside the hospital is a life-sized sculpture of a bench, and on the bench a cast bronze mother sits nursing her child. I touch it, the child.

My hand hasn't changed; it is trembling slightly, but it

still fits a baby's head.

An older woman rounds the bench and sits down on it. She nods at me.

"Visiting here?" she asks.

"Not really. I live here now."

She smiles kindly. "I meant the hospital. You have someone here?" She points with her chin at the sculpture child. "A little one?"

"Oh. I guess I do. She had an accident."

"Well, then, I'm sorry. I hope she is okay." She pulls a sandwich out of her bag and takes a bite, then she pulls out a length of yarn. As she picks up her crochet hook, an ambulance rushes by.

"She's fine," I say. "Thanks."

"My sister was in an accident, bad, when we were kids. She was okay, too. But you wonder how she would've been without that. Maybe braver; you never know."

I imagine her sister, a subdued woman in her sixties. "As long as she came out of it fine."

"Oh, she's not so good now after all. Drugs and stuff. Problems." She looks out at University Avenue traffic as she talks.

My fingers have found the baby's head again. My little finger pulses on a breast.

The woman says, "You try to help. After a while you realize there's only so much you can do." She chews as she regards me. "But you're young. Your daughter will still need you for a long time."

"My daughter . . ." I say.

What could Asha need from me?

36

MONDAY. I head outside to run errands for Father Jerome. He offered his requests cautiously after yesterday's hospital visit, extending a kindness to take me through the coming weekday. But when I glanced at him as I pushed open the door today, I saw that he would be relieved if I walked out and did not return.

Harold is sitting on the rectory stairs when I come back with Father Jerome's dry cleaning. The suit jacket is heavy in my hand. I hold it high with aching muscles, sweat cooling my sides.

The garment drapes from a paper-wrapped hanger. It is covered with a shroud of clingy plastic, under whose sheen the black wool appears seamless and rich. The details vanish into the dark depths.

Harold's anguish is as deep, an ocean behind sallow eyes.

Have ever anyone's eyes drawn me down to them before? I sit beside Harold and lay the suit jacket across our laps.

Clouds close over the sun, then release it. Cloud, then sun. When the wind billows under the plastic covering, I place my hands on top, settling it, and Harold does the same.

God preserve us, people say. As though to exist, unchanging, is enough.

Harold and I sit preserved, pickled in our tissue-thin plastic. The dark suit seems to shift across our legs like black brine. Our hands float on top, palms damp, petrifying in salt.

I lift my hand. The plastic drops away. I take Harold's fingers in my own. With the other hand, I lift the dry cleaning off our laps. Then I rise and grip Harold's arm. His biceps seem shrunken, his bones a feeble frame for his stretched-out overcoat.

The front door is heavier than usual, but Harold is light in my hands. I lead him in. As we climb the stairs, I imagine him drifting upward and bumping on the ceiling.

("Mommy, how come God let Jesus walk on water but he would let me drown?")

I draw a bath, hot. Scalding pinpricks splash my cheeks. Then I rise to retrieve Harold from where he slumps on the toilet lid.

He is easy to peel. Layers fall from him like sheets of skin. Coat. The old, satin lining catches on the burrs of Harold's parched hands. Shirt, wrinkled and unwashed. Buttons release under my coaxing; a line of empty, open holes like misshapen mouths tumble down his belly. I draw his sweaty T-shirt up over his face, over his head. His gaze is cast down, low on my body in front of him.

Here is his buckle. I open it. Draw down the zipper. Draw down my body. Draw down the stale work pants, the nubbly socks. Harold puts his hands on my shoulders, balancing to step out of clothing. For a moment I think it is I who am naked.

I guide him to the water as a mother guides a son, as a daughter guides a grandfather.

When Harold has sunk deep into the bath, gasping at the heat, I slip away to the kitchen. Perhaps the cupboards hold cures. My hand closes on a blind, squeezable bear full of honey. I carry it up the stairs and into the thick steam.

Here lies Harold, wide and scalded, lips open and eyes closed. The bear in my hand mocks me with its red cap and yellow nozzle, but as I grip it, it softens and warms. It will be enough.

Kneeling, I squeeze its round body. Honey oozes in an unbroken, sticky stream into the bathwater between Harold's feet. I glance up, past his white legs, past the dark hairs that undulate around his penis and creep up his chest. His face is expressionless. Frustration stings my eyes.

My hands swirl the shimmering honey into the bathwater.

The man I wash is a blank. Skin bare, thoughts unknown, eyes closed, and eyelids still.

Wake to me, Harold.

Deep crevices run down each cheek. They are soft to my touch. They frame lips that seem to fall forever. The heart within this soft chest, somewhere between these smooth, tiny nipples, is deeply hidden, its yearnings suffocated and buried.

Wake to me, Harold. Wake to me.

I remove my layers of clothing and leave them crumpled over Harold's on the bathroom floor. I enter the musty, sweet water and lay myself down. Belly to belly, nipples folded against nipples, I melt into Harold's body.

The lids of his eyes clamp down in a tight grimace. I lift a hand to stroke them. Lids, lashes, bristling eyebrows. I feel my own brow muscles release.

I sigh, and Harold looks at me.

His eyes are dark. His arms come up and hold me.

("There were three in the bed,
And the little one said,
'Roll over . . . '")

The bathwater is hot. My lungs fill with steam. Warm, soft, the steam in this shrinking room fills me. My ribs rise, my diaphragm draws down, my belly presses against Harold's.

I have forgotten how to breathe. It hurts to breathe.

I breathe.

I breathe out sound and pain. I hear Harold's breath in my skin, against my ears, licking past me, passing.

Our breath rises in the steam. It condenses on the walls. Rivulets on the tile walls, on my cheeks, salt water on my lips. Harold's mouth is gentle, lifting to mine. Our mouths open into a single common breath, a sigh of regret lingering like lake fog in the air.

A stroke of sunlight quivers on Harold's brow.

When the water gets cold, I pull the plug and switch on the shower. The first buckshot blast hits.

Harold and I sit on the bottom of the emptying tub. We lather and scrub in the warm, pelting rain.

I keep Harold with me this night, nestling his bulk into my cot-like bed. I sleep on him and around him. In the morning I bring him breakfast, then release him to the outside world.

He pauses on the front porch.

"I never told you about my sister Enid," he says.

"It's all right. You don't have to."

"She has a happy life," he says.

"Good." I reach out and give his hand a squeeze.

"I think she has a happy life."

"It's hard to know, isn't it?"

"You can't know," he says.

"Have you ever asked her?"

He smiles a little. I wonder if it was always there, that sadness in his smile.

He walks off the porch with his familiar gait. I notice with an ache that his arms hang loose when he walks, loose and low, barely swinging. I wish I could tuck his arms around him.

He walks off the porch, and a bit of my barely minted hope leaves with him.

37

I HAVE TAKEN TO HANGING AROUND Father Jerome's office. It is not the first time that chores have seemed pointless, but this time it is different. I flit around with a dust mop or broom here and there. I waft around in a show of cleaning.

Matthilda is resting at home now. They released her reluctantly from the hospital. The nurses would have liked to keep her longer, not for the sake of further recovery but because they loved her calm nature, her careful drawings, and the chains of paper dolls she spent hours cutting and colouring. Matthilda taped the chains together, Patsy says, making one unbroken thread of changing paper dolls which the nurses wove in and out of her bed rails.

Patsy comes in occasionally, but she has somewhere else to be these days. She is tending to Matthilda carefully, reshaping her while she has a chance. Matthilda always loved to create things; I see, now, that she got that from Patsy.

Father Jerome heads out after breakfast.

"Even priests go for coffee," he says. "Priests have friends. *Heh heh*. Priest friends."

When he returns, he is brimming with a brainstorm snitched from the priest at St. Brigitte's.

"You'll love this, Patsy. We're going to clothe all the young children in matching dress for their First Communion! The boys in satin robes with long monks' hoods draped down their backs. The girls in glossy white robes with wide collars."

He sits in her office and tries to talk her into the idea.

"They call them pilgrim collars," he says.

I picture the design immediately. The girls will look like carolling angels. I picture them holding open songbooks on open palms, standing straight with open mouths.

"The pilgrims weren't Catholic," Patsy points out.

"I know that. It's only fashion! I've seen how it looks; it looks great. Like a children's graduation."

Across the hall, I swivel in Father Jerome's chair, listening and scanning the bookshelves. Every once in a while I reach out with my feather duster and jiggle its tip at a spine or the edge of a shelf. Patsy and Father Jerome ignore me, even when my chair squeaks.

Patsy's voice is stony. I can almost see her imagining Matthilda a few years from now, walking the aisle in one of the simple satin robes instead of a thoughtfully chosen, carefully fitted white dress.

Father Jerome begins to plead in an authoritative way, but Patsy brushes him off.

"Let's be reasonable, Father. Think of the cost. There's all that fabric. There's the work. Someone has to get the material and supplies. Someone has to sew the gowns. Someone has to dry clean them when the parents return them. How will we pay for everything?"

"We'll charge!" he says. "We'll rent them for—"

"Rent them out, Father?" I can hear her eyebrows ratchet up.

"Well, okay, not rent them. But those who can afford it will make a donation, I'm sure."

Patsy's not sure. She's getting fed up with the reticence of those who can afford it.

Father Jerome pushes harder. "But really, Patsy! How will it look if we keep parading our typical mishmash of clothing when the children at St. Brigitte's are going to be so ship-shape?"

When Patsy doesn't respond, I glance at her across the hall. Her expression suggests she is coming around. She blinks like a cartoon character. She looks almost cute. Then she turns her head toward me. Her eyes focus below my face.

"Fine, then, Father," she says slowly. Challenge swells in her voice. "If you want robes, let's get some done up right away.

"It will be a job for Marta."

For a moment, no one says anything. Then Patsy smiles and looks up at me. Her eyebrows are raised.

At last Father Jerome speaks. "Well." He sighs. "You know, Patsy, I'm sure you could find someone in the neighbourhood who does these things. In fact, I'm certain that if you ask around . . . We could make an announcement about it, a call for service actually. It will be our sewing ministry. You never know but that someone has been wanting to put their talents to use for the church. It could be that someone's been waiting to be asked."

"Like Marta, for instance," Patsy interjects. "As a way of repaying you for your kindness."

A growl rumbles behind my teeth.

Patsy knows I will refuse; I can see it in her face. She waits to hear me protest the amount of labour, the expense, the trouble. No need for Patsy to argue with the good Father. Just put it to Marta and let her shoot down the plans.

Patsy knows I can sew. She knows too, somehow, that I don't wish to. But there is much Patsy does not know. How my bloodlines were drawn and torn in thread. How with every step on the sidewalk my foot pierces fabric, emerges and pierces. That my fingers find themselves ready, pinched together against an invisible needle, drawing thread through the air near my hipbone as I walk, hand-sewing—

("You see, Marta? It's as though the needle were a little swimming creature. In and out, pull up and take a breath, and now in and out . . .")

My body knows the motions like a parent knows her child. The act hovers around me always, a part of me: phantom limbs tethered close yet always in the way. I will not unleash them for the sake of memory. I will not live out my mother's legacy, but perhaps I can create my own.

Father Jerome is mortified. "Patsy," he says, "what on earth are you thinking?"

"I know what she's thinking," I say. They both stare at me. "She's thinking I'm the only one who would do it right." Patsy looks surprised, almost alarmed. "She's thinking that Matthilda will have her First Communion one day, and she wants her to look beautiful." I smile. My smile says, *I understand.* "Matthilda is such a pretty girl, and it's such an important event."

Father Jerome nods. "Very important. That's right. Very important indeed."

I go on. "All the more reason to make sure that every one of the little children looks lovely and presentable."

"You mean," Father Jerome glances from me to Patsy and back again, "you *like* the idea of putting them all in matching gowns?"

I nod. "How could anyone not like it? It sounds as though the way it is now, some children look like royalty, while others are in hand-me-downs. That doesn't seem right. Isn't every one of those kids equal and important—"

"In the eyes of God?" Father Jerome's voice quavers with excitement.

"In your eyes, Father. In Patsy's eyes."

Patsy moistens her lips. Her eyes look worried.

"I'll make some lunch," I say.

I leave Patsy's eyes that way.

∞

I cook for Father Jerome while Patsy does paperwork in the office. When he has gone up to his room, before I've even cleared the table, Patsy appears. She hesitates in the doorway as though she's uncomfortable in the kitchen. I realize, in that moment, that this kitchen has become mine.

I pour two cups of coffee and set them on the table.

(*"You'll never learn to sew properly if you don't concentrate, Marta."*

"I am concentrating, Mama! You're going too fast."

"Well, then, what part did you miss?"

"I don't know what I missed. Can't you just tell me?"

"No. I can't. Work it out for yourself.")

Patsy's face seems to be decomposing. There is a slackness, a falling of her cheeks. Something in her eyes reminds me that they rest in bone-encircled holes.

"Can we talk?" she asks.

"Of course," I say, and she sits. I am feeling benevolent: Say all you want. I am here to listen. *Heh heh.* I can almost feel the chuckle twitch through me.

She stares at her coffee, her hands in her lap. I lift mine and drink. The flavour is rich and intense. The heat is satisfying.

"You surprised me," Patsy says.

"Yes, I know."

"I don't want Matthilda wearing a rental gown."

"I know. You think it's one of the worst things that could happen to her, right?"

She tilts her head. She doesn't like me.

I add, "But not because Matthilda is better than the other kids. Not because she's special." I pause. "Even though she truly is."

Patsy's expression turns quizzical, almost confused. She brings her elbows up onto the table. Her fingers weave together. "Special?" she repeats, her voice straining against her knuckles.

I lift my mug and our eyes meet over our hands.

Her voice drops. "Is she really, Marta?" She hesitates. "Is Matthilda special?"

It must be hard for her to ask me, to have to ask the nanny. I say gently, "You really don't know?"

She looks away. "Maybe I never thought about it."

"About her, you mean. You never gave her much thought."

Patsy lifts her chin. "I thought about her, Marta. Of course I think of her. I always thought she was quite good. Better behaved than other children. Frankly, she was much better before. Before you came on the scene."

My voice hardens. "She was more compliant."

Patsy squints in surprise: I have used a big word.

"More obedient," I say. "Less trouble."

She nods.

"An easy child," I say.

She nods again. A grateful smile nudges the edges of her lips.

I touch my fingertips together. "Easy to what? To leave alone to amuse herself? To neglect while you were busy with someone more difficult?"

Patsy's face blanches to the colour of the steam that drifts up from her black coffee.

I press on. "Easy to entrust to someone you can't stand?"

She rises out of her chair, setting the wooden legs clattering and the coffee rocking sharply in its cup.

"That's enough!" she snaps.

"When did she stop being so easy?" I ask. "When she started having secrets with someone other than herself? When she started speaking up for herself? When I became her friend? How long did you think you could ignore her?"

Patsy whirls around and grabs the back of the chair. Rings jut from her fingers.

"There will always be needy parishioners, Patsy."

Her arms are shaking. Her bracelets patter like metal rain.

I place my fingers on the rim of my cup. I take a deep breath.

"Patsy," I say, "I had a daughter, too. She was special, like Matthilda. She died when she was five."

Patsy's lips drop open.

I get up. I fetch the dishcloth that is draped over the tap and wipe up Patsy's spilled coffee. As I turn to toss the cloth back, she sinks into her chair.

"I didn't know," she says. She looks horrified.

I nod. "She burned to death."

Patsy wraps her hands around her coffee. Without taking her eyes from my face, she draws the mug close to her chest.

"My daughter," I say, "was also easy."

Patsy bites her lip. I wait for her to ask me to go on.

Finally she says quietly, "Easy to . . .?"

I look for Asha inside my heart. I listen for her there. I feel her, but she is silent.

"To remember," I say. "Every moment. Every day. Everything she ever said. Everything she ever did."

Patsy's eyes brim with concern.

"Everything I did with her," I say. "And, especially, everything I didn't do. I remember."

Patsy's fingers loosen on her coffee cup. They slip to the table.

I reach across and cover them.

When I hear Father Jerome's footsteps approaching, I let go of Patsy's hands. She doesn't raise her eyes when he enters the kitchen, or while he stands there looking back and forth from her curved spine and lowered head to my upturned face that reveals nothing.

"Marta," he says, "about the Communion gowns."

"You don't have a sewing machine here," I say.

"No. And anyway, I . . ."

"And people don't like to lend their machines. Because of, you know, the tension."

That throws him off. His voice swoops slightly. "The tension?"

"The thread tension. It's so hard to get it right after someone's fiddled with it."

"Oh."

"Also," I add, "because it's a *thing,* you know?"

He shakes his head a little. He glances at Patsy, but she isn't making any moves to help him. "It's a thing?"

"A sewing machine. It's one of those *things* that even if you never touch it, as soon as it leaves you, you realize that you can't live without it. Right away you need it back, and—"

"Oh!" he says. "I know exactly what you mean! It's like some of my books," he begins eagerly. He reaches behind him to pull up a chair and join us. Then he realizes that there are only two chairs. His eyebrows draw together in consternation.

"Marta," he says slowly, "why are there only two chairs in the kitchen?"

"There always were just two chairs, Father."

He stares at me stupidly.

"I eat when you're not around," I explain. "Like Harold. Like Matthilda."

I look at Patsy, at the stiffly curled bangs that block my view of her eyes.

"Father," I ask, "where are these books of yours? Somewhere in your office, maybe? I've never seen anything very interesting in your room."

"In my room? No. My bedroom is like a desert. Or perhaps an early garden. A place to pray. To till and weed and—"

"Plant?"

He thinks about that. "One's bedroom, if one can help it, should be empty, don't you think?"

Yes. I do.

I realize that I do.

∞

In my house in Restive, my mother's portable sewing machine sits on the floor of the closet under the stairs.

Garments hang down over it. Female garments, my garments. They conceal the handle of its case and disturb the dust on its rectangular top. Many times I have opened that closet door, leaned against clothing, shoved years of clothes apart to contemplate a single item: striped blazer, wraparound skirt, spaghetti-strapped summer dress. The collection splitting open like reluctant thighs. Metal hangers squealing on the metal rod. Occasionally a moth puckering out and disappearing.

I should cover these clothes, should get rid of this, does anything here even fit me, do I fit anywhere here?—all this was pressed into the dark triangle of closet.

If only it were all gone. All its people are gone, and still the house in Restive crowds in on me. Its contents press on me still.

∞

Father Jerome is picking at his fingertips. I can see the raw skin and the broken bits like tiny flags. I can feel his desire to take his ragged fingerprints between his teeth.

"I'm still not fully certain," he says. "I don't believe I understand your feelings about the gowns."

"What do you want to know?" Why shouldn't he ask? I want the words to burst from his lips: *Do you, Marta, take—*

He clears his throat. "Well, will you . . . are you willing to . . . sew the First Communion gowns for us?"

His eyes flit to his fingers. Patsy watches me steadily from under her bangs.

"Yes," I say.

Patsy leans back, exhaling. She looks exhausted. She does, I admit, look like me.

I expect Father Jerome to cheer. Instead, the centre of his mouth curves up in an inverted smile.

"Huh," he says.

38

So now I will sew the gowns, a collection of perfect robes, and one day Matthilda will wear one of them. By then, the garment will be far past the pristine vision of Father Jerome or the standards of Patsy Wallace. Matthilda will wear it my way then: imperfect, its gloss punctuated by pulled threads and stubborn stains, the hem loose or ringed by a rim of dirt.

I will put something inside each hem.

I will tuck something into the fold of unfinished fabric at each garment's vulnerable bottom edge, then press the fabric over and into itself, and seal it shut.

I will work the needle along the fabric, inscribing the wide circle of hem with a line of stitching: holding it up, holding it closed, punctuating it with dots and dashes of thread, laying out my signature in Morse code.

I will wait, each spring, year after year, as the children struggle up the aisle in two parallel lines, catching hems on heels and nervous giggles in throats.

Then one year, when the children try on their gowns in anticipation of the day, someone's stitching will let go. A hem will drop its long-hidden treasure. That will be the beginning, then.

The children, with their perfect radars trained on things secret or destructing, won't overlook the tiny catastrophes. They'll tug further at the slovenly hems. They'll bend to pick up the strange, tiny gifts and never, I am certain, tell anyone of their finds. That is how magic sneaks through the cracks of this world.

One child will receive the slivers of a five-dollar bill. Another, a line of beads. One, a thin silver-coloured chain. Another, a slim braid of hair.

I can't say what Matthilda will get; fate will decide.

In one gown, indistinguishable from the rest, I will sew in a piece of paper, a pencilled message on a pencil-thin slip: *believe*. And on the other side, tight letters pushing against the speed bumps of the writing on the back, I will continue, or begin: *in despair*.

What message will flutter down with the unravelling of heel-scuffed thread? *Believe in despair?* Or *In despair, believe?*

A slice of photo. A single lash. A drying blade of grass. A length of lace edging from Asha's pink dress.

Ribbons of words cut from the Bible, strung together—*the spirits of the dead tremble in the waters under the earth my life is disappearing like smoke my body is burning like fire I hear the roar of rain approaching*—with dots of glue like lost baby teeth.

The choice of passages won't matter. Their meaning is in the weight of scissors in the hand.

I will wield the needle like a knife, like the shard of metal it is. Slice into the weave; force the point. Wrench the warp from the weft, push the needle through the emptiness I create.

Tug. Bind fabric to fabric. *Do you, Marta, take.*

I will hold the needle like a pen. Draw an ink of thread between pages. Pierce together the stories. Blanket stitch. Whip stitch. Running stitch. Baste.

I will baste.

I will baste because the story always turns and mocks me. I will let the heat be in the machine, let the power be under my foot. I will press the pedal and run the story down.

Dear Asha,

Moving forward. Is this what you have done, too?

How can forward lead to you, when you are always here in me? How can I say of you "was"? Are you not with me now: Am I not your mother still?

Patsy's office is empty. The top of her desk holds an empty in-basket and the phone.

I dial from memory, but don't manage to recall the sound of my father's voice before I hear his soft "Hello."

"It's me." Suddenly I feel very tired.

"Marta. Is everything all right?"

"Pretty much."

There are a few moments of silence, which my father, typically, does not feel the need to break.

"The old lady died," I say. "Mrs. Oland."

"I'm sorry to hear that. It sounds as though she was a lovely person. Your friend spoke very highly of her."

"Lawrence Edgar."

"That's right."

"What else did he say?"

"Oh, I don't know. Not a lot. He called a few times, I suppose to let me know you were okay. I appreciate that, Marta."

"Papa, I'm sorry, but I didn't ask him to call you."

Another pause. Then, "I guess I knew that. It's all right. Sometimes friends know what friends need, even without their asking."

"Lawrence isn't my friend. He was snooping. He was suspicious."

"Of you? That's very strange. But I should have guessed. He seemed surprised when I mentioned your living in Restive."

I press my fingertips into my scalp. "He didn't know anything about my family. No one here did. That's how I wanted it."

Again there is a pause. My father says quietly, "I don't mind being a house painter."

For a moment, I'm stymied. Then I realize. Of course: He still thinks of my family as *him*. "I'm not ashamed of you, Papa. I wouldn't hide you from anyone."

But I had: I'd hidden him from my daughter. I no longer understand why.

He exhales slowly. My eyes close, and I hear the waves he used to describe for me, I feel the warmth of the beach to which he used to transport me on words alone.

(*"Your body is heavy."*)

"You disappeared," he says.

(*"Like water sinking deep into sand."*)

"I called and called. You never answered.

"So I went looking for you in Restive. No one knew what had happened to you.

"And then that man phoned. He said, 'Are you a relation of Marta Fett?' And my heart—" His voice catches. "You don't know how it feels when . . ."

The word fades into a long silence.

Then I whisper, "Papa, I do know."

And he answers, softer than ever. "Yes. I know you do."

Far away, in the kitchen of my old home in Kingston, with a faint scrape, Papa pulls up a chair. We sit mouth to ear and I listen to him, listen like a child held in a lap in a rocking chair.

"Marta, do you remember the cheque I sent you, years ago, from your mother?"

"Yes."

"It was none of my business what you did with it, and I knew you didn't want me to prod, but under the circumstances . . . I waited a long while without hearing from you. Then I phoned to discuss your plans for the money, and your future. Kurt answered."

"You told him about the cheque?"

"No, I didn't. But he told me that you were expecting."

Aim, thrust, *twist*. Papa had known all along. He'd heard it from Kurt. He knew. "I've got to go."

"But— Okay. Will you call me soon?"

"No. I don't know."

"Wait."

"No."

"Marta, please! Five years I've waited to hear from you."

"I can't explain."

"All Kurt said was that you were pregnant. And that you didn't want me to know."

I let the line fall silent again, and this time, for the first time, I feel his anguish in the vacuum.

He says, "It's all right. I learned a long time ago that you can't make someone love you."

My heart aches. "It wasn't that."

"Will you do something for me? Please don't hang up," his quiet voice quakes. "Please tell me, my Marta. Tell me all about the girl. Your daughter."

"Papa." I choke on the words. "Maybe it's better not to know."

"Please. Tell me about my granddaughter."

Tears well up and blind me. They slide from my eyes to the phone in my hands.

I whisper unsteadily, "Did you know her name?"

"I do know. Of course I do."

"But how do you know?"

"Marta, it was in the paper."

"The paper?"

"I read it in the newspaper."

"I didn't. Read it." It seems so strange. My daughter in the paper.

"Asha," he sighs.

I nod gratefully.

"Her name is Asha," he says, as if he could never forget.

39

THE SUN, drawn to the warmth of the porch stairs, dries my lashes and face and soothes my blotchy skin. After a while, I climb up and crawl across the dusty wooden planks to the shady part of the porch. I lie down because Matthilda once said to. She was right. It feels nice.

Footsteps slap the sidewalk and I turn my head to watch Harold. He clomps up the stairs.

"Hey, Marta. Hear you're going to do a sewing job."

"Mmm." I lift onto my elbows.

"You need any help with it?"

"You could help me get my stuff into a cab if you're around."

"Sure. Just tell me the day before. I'll be pretty busy. Lots of rectory work coming up."

"Says who?"

"Father Jerome."

"Really? That's great."

"I'm a good worker, Marta. You don't have to sound so shocked."

I laugh as I sit up. I take Harold's hand and squeeze it. "You're right, Harold. You're a good man."

∾

Patsy's shadow falls into the eternal semi-darkness of my small room. I am sitting on the bed, knees up, feet crossed, with my back against the wall and a pen in my hand. There is little else to do in this room. I've never minded that.

"Come on in," I say, and Patsy enters. She didn't expect to sit on the bed with me, but after turning this way and that and finding no chair and no wall space to lean against, she accepts my gestured invitation and sits.

"Are you writing?" she asks. "It's dark in here for that."

She surprises me. I thought she believed me illiterate. Then I realize how ridiculous I've been. Would she have sent me to help Mrs. Oland if she thought I couldn't address packages?

I smile. "Not really. I've got the pen and paper but it seems I can really only write in my head."

"You write stories?"

"Sort of letters."

Slowly, she repositions herself on the bed. "I like to write letters," she says thoughtfully, "but not in my head. Sometimes it feels as though the words are only in my hands."

I think about that. "Father Jerome used to write," I say. "Harold mentioned it. I assumed he meant stories. I wonder if he's kept at it."

"As a priest? I doubt it. He's not allowed to reveal what his parishioners tell him, and what else is there for him? How could he ever write a word when there's so much he simply can't say? Maybe it's better your way. All in your head."

I laugh a low grunt of a laugh. "Believe me, it's not on purpose."

Patsy looks down. "Is anything ever?"

When I don't reply, she raises her eyes to mine.

"You're going to sew the gowns," she says.

"Yes."

"It's a big job."

"I suppose so."

"It could take a long time. It could take you away from us for a while."

It is a question. "Yes," I say. I feel her exhalation in the movement of the bedsprings.

"So you're going to sew them somewhere else."

"Yes. I have a place in mind." In the dim light I see her considering this: Marta knows a place, has a place, a place beyond the rectory.

Patsy stands. "Then I guess I should get you some money. For the material." She faces me, wringing her fingers, rubbing her knuckles with her thumbs. Her eyes remind me of Father Jerome's as he held his weights in the air.

"Patsy," I say, "I'm not leaving yet. You can get me the money tomorrow. I'll find out exactly what Father Jerome has in mind for the fabric."

She remains standing. She licks her lower lip, then draws it in and holds it between her teeth.

"Anyway," I continue, "I should buy the supplies in Toronto. There's a great fabric store in the west end."

"Oh, there is? Lovely," she says. "That should be fine, then." Her voice is weak, false.

She turns to leave. I get off the bed quickly, startling her. Her hand swings out as if in defence.

"Would you like to come with me?" I ask. "To the fabric

store? It'll be an adventure."

I can't believe what I'm saying to Patsy Wallace. Neither can she, but she nods. We stare at each other. All I know is what Harold told me: You can't know.

∾

There is still Matthilda.

"She's different," Patsy tells me on the subway. "She's quieter now."

"Like before?"

"No, not like before. Not shy or frightened. Just quieter. Like she's thinking about things."

"Calmer."

"Yes, calmer. And something else. Changed, somehow."

"Saved."

Patsy looks alarmed.

"I mean you've saved her," I say. "You showed her that you love her. She'll be fine now. Once you've been saved, you can't go back."

The subway train brakes suddenly, and Patsy's body is pushed against mine. I think of my high school days: bare legs and sports uniforms, huddling with the girls' basketball team before the game, our hands piled over each other as we prayed to win, hands pressing down on hands, held up by the bottom hand, by the girl resting hers on nothing.

We right ourselves.

"Do you really think Matthilda has been saved?" Patsy asks.

"Unless there's another word for it."

If there is, I haven't learned it yet.

40

BACK AT THE RECTORY, we each take the end of a bolt and huff up the stairs and into the empty front room. We have bought two whole bolts of fabric, Patsy and I. We have bought thread, lots of thread. I shake a bag upside down and more spools of thread tumble out. They spin across the floor. Patsy fishes into another bag and draws out lining, interfacing, zippers and buttons. She places the bag on the floor and lays our purchases on top of it. The buttons are attached with bent wires to small cardboard rectangles. We are rich with cardboard rectangles dangling pearly buttons.

"How will you manage with all this?" Patsy asks.

"You can take anything on a bus. I'll grab taxis to and from the stations."

Patsy crouches over the small hill of button cards. She picks one up and starts pulling apart the wires.

"No point in carrying all this cardboard, is there?" She doesn't wait for an answer. The first button drops into her hand. I see that she'd like to touch it to her lips, to feel its silkiness there.

I sit down beside her and put a handful of cards in my lap.

"Perhaps it will be okay," Patsy says.

"What?"

"The gowns. Matthilda in a gown, a rental gown."

I pretend to think hard. "You know," I say, "I could put one aside for a few years. Until it's Matthilda's turn. Pull it out just for her, when the time comes, and it'll be brand spanking new."

Patsy's eyes light up briefly before she catches the teasing tone in my voice. To her credit, she shrugs and smiles. "It's all right," she says. "We'll take what we get."

"Anyway, who knows if you'll even be at St. Boniface then? It's a few years down the road. Anything could happen."

Patsy picks more buttons off in silence. Then she looks at me. "Do you really think so, Marta?"

"What?"

"Can anything really happen?"

"Sure," I say. "It happens all the time."

When we've finished stripping all the cards, I push my fingers into our pile of buttons and scoop up a small handful. I lay a few down, side by side, then keep going. I line them all up beside each other in a gleaming path that meanders across the floor. On impulse I hand the last few buttons to Patsy. She bites her lip and finishes the job.

I grin at her. She smiles sheepishly.

"Time to start dinner," I say.

I leave Patsy standing over our collection, wondering, worrying, or waiting.

✑

Patsy comes down to the kitchen with a button in her palm.

"Perhaps I'll give one to Matthilda," she says, "when I tell her what you're up to."

"Yes," I say. "Every child should have buttons."

I wonder if Patsy realizes what she is giving her daughter. A single pearly button, as telling as a book.

Patsy taps the floor behind her with the toe of one shoe. "You know you don't have to sew the gowns," she says.

"Now you tell me. Oh, well. There are no returns on fabric."

"There aren't?"

I smile. "There aren't."

"But you will come back," says Patsy.

"Of course. I'll have gowns to deliver."

"And Matthilda will want to see you."

I lay my knife down beside the carrots I've been slicing. I wipe my palms on my pants and cross my arms. I lean against the counter. The tap drips behind me. "She wouldn't want to see me now?"

Patsy opens her hand and looks at the iridescent button. "No," she says quietly.

The tiny word flares in my head. "You seem to forget that you're the one who put us together. You can't blame me if she likes me."

Her voice stays soft. "I know that, Marta. And of course I wanted her to like you. But I didn't expect her to like you that much. You changed her. Or she changed for you."

"She loves me," I say.

"You did a good job. I don't regret asking you to watch her. Maybe in some ways I do. But if it weren't for you . . ."

"Then let me see her before I go."

Patsy shakes her head. "I can't let her be with you yet. Things are lovely between us now; I didn't know it could be like this. But it's new for us." She rolls her wedding ring for a moment. "It's sort of tender. I'm sorry, Marta. I can't jeopardize it now."

"You want her to yourself for a while." I realize I understand this. I wish I didn't, but I do. My whole heart understands it.

Patsy nods.

"And are you getting what you want? Is she there for you?" I try to keep the sneer out of my voice. It is, after all, a question worth asking.

"She can't go far, can she?" Patsy retorts. Her eyes are bright above her flushing cheeks.

I cluck. "You're getting sassy. I can see where Matthilda gets it from." I grin a little.

Patsy's face opens into delight. "Do you think so?" she asks. A smile plumps her cheeks. Her teeth are white and even. "Do you really think she gets something from me?"

I laugh.

"I'll come back," I say. "I'll see Matthilda then. Don't spoil her, Patsy."

41

AND SO MY TASK TAKES ME HOME. It seems impossible, but suddenly it is as easy as that.

A bus rushes me up the rural reaches of the Humber River. I sit turned toward the window with my knees up and one shoulder pressed into the upholstery.

Five months ago I expected my bus seat to slice open and swallow me whole. Now I feel it yield slightly to the solidity of my bones and I think, *My arms are strong. I can carry what I need.*

Kurt's duffle bag is bunched beside my feet. The box with the fabric is in the storage compartment in the belly of the bus, Matthilda's unfinished scarf folded on top of the lining. I have left all else behind. My bag is empty, just the way I found it.

I am hurtling home, clutching nothing.

In minutes I will turn the lock. The keys in my pocket press into the muscle of my thigh.

The sun is setting. It shines up at me, bounces up from the roofs of cars. I close my eyes and imagine my hands on the satin, steadying it on the slippery metal of the sewing machine, piercing it slowly with the needle. I imagine placing my fingertips down.

Wait. Do not push. Let the machine take the fabric.

I open my eyes and watch the landscape creating itself: the horizon running into the distance, the road racing toward me like a seam.

∞

Dear Asha,

I've loved you for a long, long time. Since the first moment I held a sleeping infant, years before you. Since before the night you were conceived in a spit of sperm and floating egg, before I pushed you into this world, before you opened your fresh, blue eyes to me, before I knew what it meant to know you. Through all your tumbled years, with their diapers and jeans and daisy shoes and budding logic and rubbing of tired earlobes with knuckles dimpled, then sturdy, then slender and spattered with ten-cent rings.

See: This is my feeble grasp of infinity, jagged with shards and objects, things long shed and forgotten by you, my sweet, my forever child.

Forgive my imperfect love, Asha. Forgive my pain. Smile on me; cradle my life in your weightless arms. Can you see it?

Here.

Acknowledgments

Warm thanks to my editor, Barbara Berson; my agent, Margaret Hart; my writers' group and those who read an early draft of this work: Helen Battersby, Leanne Lieberman, Dianne Scott, Elsie Sze, and George Hogg. Special thanks to George for over ten years of reading.

For invaluable encouragement in the beginning stages, I'm indebted to Nino Ricci, Anne Michaels, Cynthia Holz, Joe Kertes, and Eddy Yanofsky. Grateful acknowledgment to the Toronto Arts Council for their award of a writers' grant.

Heartfelt gratitude to Eduarda Sousa, Ellen Irving, and Angela Embree for faith, food, and the loan of a place to write.

For their wisdom, patience, trust, and love, I thank Bruce, Ela, and Luke Hefler.

And for everything that brought me to this, my thanks to my wonderful mom, Daniela Szado.

A Penguin Readers Guide

ABOUT THE BOOK

Written with incredible skill and sensitivity, Ania Szado's remarkable debut novel, *Beginning of Was,* takes the reader on a journey filled with love, heartache, and a search for forgiveness. It follows the life of Marta Fett from naive nine-year-old who sits at the knee of her seamstress mother to grieving twenty-six-year-old mother and widow.

When Marta was a young girl her mother abandoned her and her father, declaring that she needed a much more exciting life than the quiet, simple one she was stuck in. It was left to Marta to run the house and feed her mute father, until he eventually broke his silence, but the damage was done. He lost the respect of his daughter, and she married one of the first men who showed her any attention, hopeful that he would take her away and she could start her life over.

Marta's chance at happiness ends up being dashed by the attractive and charismatic Kurt, who quickly shows his true colours with a barrage of cruel words and neglect. The new life that grows secretly within her becomes her only ray of hope, and with the birth of Asha comes an all-encompassing love that Marta has never known. She revels in motherhood and dedicates every waking moment to Asha, soaking in each word and movement, holding her so close they are almost one being.

But Kurt's abuse and drunken rages become unbearable, and Marta makes plans to leave with Asha. However, in a horrible twist of fate, her beloved daughter is killed in a car accident that also claims the life of Kurt. Heartbroken, Marta continues with her plan, leaving her home, her belongings, and her identity as she climbs aboard a bus destined for Toronto. This is a trip she'd planned months in advance, but one she never imagined she'd do alone.

Numb with grief, Marta arrives in Toronto and lands on the steps of St. Boniface Church, where she is welcomed into the fold and even given several jobs. One of which is to help the elderly Mrs. Oland send out her valued possessions to friends and family in anticipation of the end drawing near. Marta is also asked to watch over a lonely, shy young girl, Matthilda, who is the same age as Asha. All of her new relationships force Marta to confront her painful memories, helping her in her struggle to define who she is, where she belongs, and how she can possibly move on.

Beginning of Was explores the utter depths of grief and how one mother copes with the loss of the greatest love of her life. ■

AN INTERVIEW WITH ANIA SZADO

Q: *Beginning of Was* is your first novel. What inspired you to write it?

An elderly relative had begun giving away her most prized possessions. I was intrigued by the choices she made, and I thought it poignant that her sense of an item's worth, imbued as it was with her memories and associations, often bore little relationship to the recipient's sense of the thing. That inspired a short story about an old woman with exaggerated confidence in her ability to influence others through the dispensation of specific treasured objects. As a foil, I brought in a young woman who had no possessions, who had lost everything. But the younger woman's story took over. Not only did it become the main thread, it came to demand novel-sized scope and commitment. ■

Q: Losing someone you love causes immense grief, but the loss of a child must be particularly unbearable. Everyone deals with grief in their own way, so how did you decide upon Marta's reaction and her journey to Toronto?

The decision to put Marta and Mrs. Oland together came first, then I had to discover how Marta came to be in that situation. I asked myself a lot of questions. What would make someone like Marta be willing—even desperate—to leave her former life behind? To retreat into near isolation? To reduce her world to the minimal stimuli offered by cleaning floors or packing boxes? To seek forgiveness and refuge? Losing her possessions would not be enough. She had to be fleeing from things profound: memories, grief, guilt, deep pain. Most of us tamp down our occasional impulse to run away from our struggles. Responsibilities and propriety keep us put, but Marta had no such barriers—plus she had the example of her mother, who left one life behind for another. So I let her try to escape her painful past. ■

Q: Marta experiences a series of losses in her life, starting with the abandonment of her mother, but she seems to try to be strong throughout it all. Was it important to you to show a great degree of inner strength in this character in spite of all the adversity she has faced?

It was important for a number of reasons, the first being that a character with the potential to move forward is generally more compelling than one who must remain a powerless victim. In Marta's case, strength comes not in spite of adversity, but in response to it, as a necessary act of self-preservation. As much as her inner strength pulls her through, I think it also comes to contribute to her pain. For example, she might have fled earlier with Asha had she allowed herself to give in to fear; she delays, in part, because she pits her strength against Kurt. We often chide ourselves for our weaknesses, as though the only way forward is through strength and force. But for someone like Marta, it can be more important to learn to go with the flow and accept what comes. She needs to become vulnerable and open, to find a way to accept the fear and promise of a future she can't control. ■

Q: While you were writing this novel, was it difficult for you to get into the mindset and emotions of a grieving mother? Does a character like Marta stay with you after you've finished writing the novel?

I didn't entirely realize what I was getting into when I decided to write about a grieving mother. But something invaluable and gut-wrenching happened: the writer Anne Michaels, one of my early mentors, held my hand to the fire. She showed me that I would have to be unflinching; I would have to be willing to fully inhabit Marta's grief, to truly *feel* my way through her pain and deliverance. So I tried. I drew on my own experiences—I'd lost my father in my teens and one of my brothers in my twenties. Returning to the intensity of those losses was very tough. But I was willing to go there because of where my own bereavement had taken me: to a belief that love has no end point. Death hasn't stopped me from loving my dad or my brother; it hasn't stopped me from feeling connected to them. I even feel, as I mature and change, that our relationships continue to grow. As I worked on the book, I held tight to that knowledge, and I wrote Marta toward it. After I finished the novel, she did stay with me for a long time. But I felt that I'd given her what she needed. In the end, I let go of her, knowing she would be fine. ■

Q: None of the marriages in the novel are particularly successful, from Marta's parents to Marta's own marriage with Kurt. Even Patsy Wallace and her husband are described as leading separate lives. How do you feel about the nature of marriage, and how did you want it represented in the novel?

Getting married is an incredible act of honour, hope, and naïveté. We put a lot of faith in ourselves, not just in our partners, when we say "I do." We promise that our feelings and commitment will remain the same forever, but people do (and should) change over the course of their lives. I've come to believe that one of the most important factors for long relationships is adaptability. I'm amazed by the amount of change that my own marriage can accommodate, not having seen such elasticity in my parents' marriage. I worry that there must be a breaking point—but I also worry about holding back in life. Twenty years into a great marriage, I still sometimes struggle to balance my own needs against those of my spousal and other familial relationships. The damaged marriages in *Beginning of Was* raise questions that reflect and extend that challenge. When, if ever, is it justified to break a promise—or, for these characters, a sacred vow? What if one person changes for the worst? What if addictions arise or lives are at risk? What if "only" happiness is at risk? ▪

Q: Your characters are so fully realized that it seems like they are people that you have met in real life. Mrs. Oland for example is so nuanced and detailed that it's easy to picture her as she carefully doles out her possessions or as she's getting her teeth flossed by Marta. Do you base your characters on people you know, or are they completely made up in your imagination?

Usually they're completely made up. Sometimes a specific aspect of a real person inspires a character, but generally the resemblance ends there. Take Mrs. Oland: the elderly relative who inspired the character did give away some possessions toward the end of her life, but she didn't speak or think like Mrs. Oland. She didn't look like her, or live in a house, or have ties with a rectory. And no flossing—she didn't even have her own teeth. ▪

Q: The act of sewing is threaded throughout the novel with snippets of conversations involving Marta and her mother. Did you or do you sew? What sort of symbolism were you hoping to convey to the reader with the sewing imagery?

Though I used to sew, my main associations with sewing involve my mother, who was a seamstress when I was young. I grew up playing with buttons, poring over pattern books in fabric stores, and learning the craft at her side. The conversations and memories in the novel could have been shaped around any other skill that a mother might pass on to a daughter—with all the pride, expectations, and disappointments this can engender—but I was bursting with the need to express how a button in the hands of a child can contain sadness or joy, how much can rest on the ability to pass a thread through the hole of a needle, how creating a tangible item from an amorphous sea of fabric can press away the panic of feeling inadequate and adrift.

As a child, I returned again and again to the mystery of how one thread in a sewing machine could capture another to create a seam. I couldn't make sense of the mechanics. That childhood brainwork may not have provided answers—I still think sewing machines are magical—but it provided the basic structural geometry of *Beginning of Was*. I think of the present day story as the top thread, the most visible one. While it's unspooling, so is the hidden story of Marta's childhood, the bottom thread. Every once in a while, something triggers the top thread to dip down and hook the bottom one—some possession of Mrs. Oland's calls forth a memory, or some emotional breakthrough lets Marta face her past. The childhood story surfaces reluctantly but relentlessly, linked always to something in the present, and together they make a chain that binds Marta's past to her present, eventually allowing her to accept herself and her life as a whole. ∎

Q: In addition to writing novels, you have also written short fiction. Do you have a different writing process when approaching short stories as compared with a novel?

When I was writing more short fiction, I felt as though the world was made of story ideas. An article, a song, a phrase—anything could start me thinking and writing, and I would run through a rough draft before the impetus could dissipate. I relied heavily on instinct for those first drafts, leaving the reshaping and rethinking for subsequent versions. Novel writing has proven to be a whole other creature. For one thing, the central idea or inspiration needs to have significant plasticity and staying power; I discard a lot of ideas because I can't imagine living with them for years. And the writing itself demands a different approach. I find it counterproductive to push out a full draft without reflecting and assessing along the way; I don't want to plow past opportunities to open the story up or to move closer to the essence of what it should be. So I work in a fluctuating pattern: I write, I step back to ask questions and drill for insights into the story and its characters, then I write again. If I'm away on a writing retreat—which is something I do on a regular basis—I'll typically work for at least fifteen hours a day. That's another thing about novel writing versus short stories: I find it demands longer stretches of solitude and concentration, and thus, greater understanding from my family and friends. ■

Q: What sort of advice would you give to those who wish to write a book of fiction?

I think a lot of people carry that wish as a secret for a long time, and some feel embarrassed at the presumptuousness of it. But writing a book of fiction is essentially just one-step-at-a-time, nose-to-grindstone work, like any other extended project. There's nothing arrogant about thinking you could take it on.

Don't talk about your story before you begin writing it—not because doing so makes you a bore, but because you run a very high risk of dulling the impetus to write it. Just start writing. Start with what you have, in any way you can, no matter how imperfect. Get words down, get feedback and help as the need arises, and keep raising your own bar.

Step back occasionally to ask yourself questions. Silence your nasty inner critic, but not your inner editor who asks "What's the purpose of this chapter?" or "Can I cut the first section and start the story here?" Ask your characters questions, too, or use any other means to expand and deepen your understanding of them. Knowing your characters well is an incredibly valuable aid to seeing how your story can or must move forward.

Whatever stage you're at—wishing to write, struggling to begin, or crafting the first or subsequent drafts—you're not alone. The world and the web are full of writers reaching out to other writers. We may work in solitude, but at times we all need some support. ■

DISCUSSION QUESTIONS

1. Discuss the opening pages of the novel. What was your reaction to the way the author began the novel with the accident scene?

2. The title of the novel, *Beginning of Was,* is so very poignant and representative of Marta's life after the accident. Discuss what the title means to you and how it relates to Marta's way of viewing her life on page 171.

3. Can you empathize with Marta's mother and her reasons for leaving? Can you understand her feeling of being trapped in motherhood and marriage?

4. What do you think of Marta's father and the way he shuts down after Merisa leaves? How does he differ from Kurt? Discuss the varying roles that men play in the novel.

5. What do you make of Marta's comment, "For what else are owned objects if not the touchstones and containers of our histories and our hopes?" (p. 50), and how does this quotation relate to Mrs. Oland, Marta's mother, and Marta herself? How do all three of these women treat their "things"?

6. How do you think Marta's abandonment as a child shaped her into the mother she became to Asha?

7. When Marta steps off the subway in Toronto, the first thing she sees is St. Boniface Church. Was this divine intervention leading her here? How much of a role does religion or God play in the novel?

8. Why do you think Marta keeps her past and the tragedy she experienced a secret from those she meets in Toronto? Do you think they would have treated her differently if they knew?

9. What do you make of the letters that Marta writes to Asha? What sort of insights do they give into her character? Why do you think the author used the epistolary format to convey Marta's thoughts?

10. In the end, Marta decides to sew the communion robes for the church. What did this symbolize to you? How has Marta changed from the woman she was when she first arrived at St. Boniface? Is she on the road to healing or is she still dealing with her initial grief?